"Am I the only one?"
she asked quietly.

"What?"

"The only Slayer? Are there more? Do they have support groups or anything?"

"There are girls," Merrick informed her, "all over the world, who are different. Who have the potential to become Slayers. But only one is chosen."

"Swell."

"See, Vampire-Kings move about, usually with one or two of their followers to lay the groundwork. They find a community, feed on it, make it their own. Usually this goads the community into a kind of paranoid frenzy, but for some reason, nobody here seems to be paying any attention. But the only ones who can face the Kings—the Slayers—"

He stopped, noticing that Buffy had raised her hand.

"What is it?"

"Do I have to take notes on this?"

Books by Richie Tankersley Cusick

VAMPIRE
FATAL SECRETS
BUFFY, THE VAMPIRE SLAYER
(a novelization based on a screenplay by Joss Whedon)
THE MALL
(Coming in mid-September 1992)

Available from ARCHWAY Paperbacks

BUFFY THE VAMPIRE SLAYER™

A novelization by
Richie Tankersley Cusick
Based on the screenplay by
Joss Whedon

AN ARCHWAY PAPERBACK
Published by POCKET BOOKS
New York   London   Toronto   Sydney   Tokyo   Singapore

AN ARCHWAY PAPERBACK *Original*

An Archway Paperback published by
POCKET BOOKS, a division of Simon & Schuster Inc.
1230 Avenue of the Americas, New York, NY 10020

ISBN: 0-671-79220-2

First Archway Paperback printing August 1992

10 9 8 7 6 5 4 3 2 1

AN ARCHWAY PAPERBACK and colophon are registered trademarks of Simon & Schuster Inc.

Printed in the U.S.A.

IL 6+

To Lisa Clancy . . .
brilliant in every sitch

Prologue

Europe in the Dark Ages

The stench of death was everywhere.

As the weary knight walked his horse slowly through the twilight, he could see that this village, like all the others he had traveled through, had been ravaged mercilessly by the plague. Bodies littered the streets, heaped side by side with rotting animal carcasses, and the gathering darkness echoed with the rumble of death carts and the screams of the dying. The knight kept to the middle of the road, careful to avoid the quarantined houses that had been marked with red crosses, and yet he could sense the frightened, suspicious looks from peasants as they scurried around him. He was relieved when he finally spotted an inn. He handed his horse over to the stableboy and went inside.

At first he thought the place was empty. But as his eyes adjusted to the darkness, he began to make out several customers drinking silently at their tables. No one spoke to him. Squinting through the gloom, he spotted a dark-haired girl standing lazily behind the bar, and as he stared at her disheveled appearance, she slowly scratched a birthmark on one bare shoulder.

"A tankard of ale, girl."

The knight threw his money onto the bar and watched as she drew the ale from a barrel. He drank deeply, then stood for a moment, considering.

"Some plague we're having, huh?"

His own words echoed around him, ghostly. Finishing his drink, he saw the barmaid pick up a candle and motion him to follow her upstairs. As they reached the doorway of his room, he grabbed her by the hip, surprised when she broke away and continued on down the hall. For a moment he peered after her, but then gave a resigned laugh and closed the door.

He didn't see the vampire behind it.

He didn't see, only two feet away from him, the skull-hollow eyes, the bloody smile so full of teeth, the peeling gray skin. And yet, as an icy chill went up his spine, the knight slowly began to turn.

"Oh, no . . ."

The vampire licked its lips. . . .

And then it sprang.

Helpless, the knight felt himself being thrust into the center of the room. For one second he struggled wildly, then screamed as the vampire buried its face deep in his neck.

Without warning, the door burst open, the lock shattering onto the floor. As the vampire spun around, it saw the barmaid in the doorway clutching a wooden stake tightly in her hand. Furious, the creature released the knight, who scuttled back, terrified, into a corner.

The challengers flew at each other. The barmaid twisted and kicked, and the vampire struck back. Snarling, it came at her again, and as they struggled, it suddenly slipped free and vanished out into the hall.

For a long moment the girl remained still, crouched on the floor. And then . . . as if slowly coming to a decision . . . she ran toward the window.

The vampire was already out the front door of the inn when it heard the sound of splintering wood. The barmaid came crashing through the shutters of the overhead window and landed on the creature, ramming the stake straight through its heart.

Silence settled heavily around her.

The street was strangely deserted.

And then . . . she heard a voice.

"The Lord giveth, and the Lord taketh away. Ashes . . . ashes . . ."

It was a strange voice, a giggling voice, and as it floated to her out of the black of night, the girl looked up.

"All fall down," the voice finished.

But it wasn't just one figure forming there in front of her out of the darkness.

As the barmaid stared, she could see them now, not just one figure, but ten or maybe more—all of them vampires—walking slowly toward her along the filthy street. And at the very front was the one who had spoken, a grinning jackal in rotted courtier's livery, ambling toward her, still giggling, as she stood and waited.

So focused was she on the vampires approaching that she didn't notice the one behind her. The one with smooth, bone-white skin. The one wearing a long coat, who gently floated up to her and was practically upon her before he spoke.

"You must forgive my servant, Amilyn. He tends to drool before supper."

The barmaid turned. The vampire smiled, almost lovingly.

"Lothos . . ." she whispered.

"You people will never learn."

She swung at him, but he caught her wrist. As Amilyn laughed, Lothos grabbed the back of the girl's head and pressed her to him in a tender embrace.

"We can't be stopped," Lothos murmured. "This is our world now."

There was only one quick jerk of his hand . . .

And then a jagged flash of lightning as the barmaid slumped lifelessly in his arms.

Outside a castle window, lightning ripped through the night sky, torrents of rain glittering eerily in the brief, flickering light. While the storm raged without, a young girl raged within, arguing hysterically with an old man.

"I can't!"

"You know you must," the old man said quietly. "There is only one. Now you are that one. It is time."

"Why? Why me?"

The old man shook his head. "She has died.

5

You are the next to be called. Why do you think you were sent to me? Trained as you were? You bear the mark."

Slowly he pulled the neck of her blouse aside to reveal a birthmark on her shoulder.

"The mark of the Order," he murmured.

"I don't understand!"

The old man's voice was solemn. "Ever since Adam and Eve first left the garden, he has followed: the serpent, the Evil One. He sends his legions in the shape of men, to feed on us, to breed his hell on our earth. They are a plague upon us."

As the girl watched, mystified, he unraveled a bundle of cloth and pulled something from it.

A wooden stake. Long and sharp and elaborately carved.

"But as long as there have been vampires," the old man went on, "there has been the Order, the line of Slayers. Ones with the strength and the skill to kill them, to find them where they gather and stop the swell of their numbers. One dies, the next is called."

"I'm just a girl!"

"You are much more."

The old man gave her the stake. To the girl's dismay, she felt the perfect fit of it, the perfect feel of it in her hand.

"One dies," the old man murmured, "the next is called. . . ."

And as she gripped the stake more tightly, a startling awareness seemed to fill her, an incredible sense of power rushing through her and overwhelming her.

Slowly . . . slowly . . . the young girl lifted the stake over her head.

Buffy lifted her hand high in the air and gave her pom-pom a shake. Following her cue, the other Hemery High cheerleaders broke into a rousing yell, and the stands echoed with the screams of enthusiastic students.

The Hemery versus Seton basketball game was in wild progress. Buffy could see Coach pacing the sidelines, shouting at the players above all the chaos, and she exchanged amused looks with her friends Jennifer and Nicole as the three of them broke into another cheer. Working effortlessly through her routines, Buffy glanced at the scoreboard and then out onto the court, trying to follow the swift maneuvers of the players. The boys seemed to be everywhere all at once—Jeffrey, the forward; Andy, the center forward; Grueller, the huge left guard—and as Seton intercepted a pass and scored two points, a massive groan went up from the crowd. Buffy winced, and the players fell back to take the ball out of bounds.

"All right, guys, come on!" Andy yelled.

The referee gave Andy the ball. As the players got into position, Jeffrey looked straight over at Buffy, and she flushed with pride. To be Jeffrey's girlfriend was to be the envy of every girl at Hemery High, and as she smiled back at him, he gave her that suave wink that never failed to melt her heart.

> *"Jeffrey! Jeffrey!*
> *He's our man!*
> *If he can't do it,*
> *We don't want it!"*

Buffy revved the cheerleaders up again, the crowd echoing their chants, louder and louder. Andy threw the ball in to Thompson, who fed it back. Jeffrey ran in circles till Andy sailed him the ball, and then, in one split instant, Jeffrey slammed the ball in for two points.

The crowd jumped to its feet, crazed with

excitement. As the cheerleaders screamed and hugged each other, Buffy did a graceful standing back flip, then straightened up again to see Nicole staring at her with an impressed nod. Buffy brushed her blond hair from her eyes and gave her friend a giddy smile. Great game . . . now on to some serious shopping, she thought.

"Mr. Howard is so heinous. He's always giving me a hard time," Buffy moaned, and glanced from side to side at her friends for sympathy. Nicole and Jennifer were intent on window-shopping, and Kimberly, who had met them here after the game, was having trouble maneuvering her heavy shopping bags through the crowds. The mall was busy today, noisy and packed with people, and as the girls made their way past the stores, Buffy tried again.

"I get a C-plus on the test, and he tells me, 'You have no sense of history.' I have no sense of history? He wears a brown tie!"

"You got a C-plus?" Nicole looked up at last. "I can't believe I cheated off you."

Buffy shook her head, disgusted. "Excuse me for not knowing about El Salvador. Like I'm ever going to Spain anyway. Ooh!"

As they paused outside a store, Buffy pulled

a dress from a display rack and held it in front of her.

"Mmmm . . . wouldn't I look just edible and nutritious in this?"

"Guys, what's the sitch? I'm bored," Kimberly complained as she and Jennifer caught up with the other two. She stopped and stared at Buffy behind the dress.

"What do you think?" Buffy asked eagerly.

"Please." Kimberly yawned. "It's so five minutes ago."

"Oh . . ." Face falling, Buffy put the dress back, and Kimberly turned and confronted the rest of the group.

"So, what are we doing?"

"Why don't we see a movie?" Buffy suggested brightening.

"Well, where?"

Jennifer thought for a minute. "Omniplex?"

"No THX." Buffy shook her head.

"They don't even have Dolby," Nicole reminded them, and Kimberly nodded.

"Beverly Center."

"Please," Buffy sighed. "They show previews for foreign movies."

"AMC?" Nicole tried.

Kimberly and Buffy rolled their eyes. "Bogus corn!" Buffy said.

"Totally stale," Kimberly agreed. "And the ushers are, like, the acne patrol."

Nicole spread her arms. "We're thinking Pavilion. Sitch?"

"Sounds toasty," Buffy said, picking up her shopping bag again. "We're going to Pavilion."

"Excellent," Jennifer echoed.

Buffy shrugged her shoulders with a quizzical smile. "What's playing there?"

She wasn't really paying attention as the strange, dark figure came toward her out of the crowd. She only felt a sudden jolt as the man bumped into her and kept on walking, without so much as a backward glance.

"Excuse much!" Buffy called after him. "Not rude or anything!"

He was an older man, about fiftyish, she guessed, and his wrinkled black suit and shirt reminded Buffy of a shabbily dressed priest.

"Nice ensemble!" Kimberly shouted, and Nicole giggled.

"What a bum," Buffy remarked.

The girls snickered and kept walking.

They didn't see the man suddenly stop and turn to gaze after them.

His intense expression was slightly worried. His face was haggard, and yet a keen intelligence shone from his eyes. He held himself stiffly, arms close to his sides, almost as though he expected something to strike at him.

He pulled a picture from his coat pocket and looked at it . . .

And then once again he stared at the girls.

Are your parents really going away for the *whole* weekend?" Nicole asked.

Buffy nodded and glanced up at the movie screen. The four of them had been so busy talking ever since they'd sat down in the theater that, it suddenly occurred to her, she didn't even know how long the film had been running.

"That's the plan," she said, smiling.

Nicole looked pleased. "Good enough!"

"Your parents are always going away for the weekend," Jennifer sighed, taking a long sip of diet soda. "You're so lucky."

Buffy hesitated. "Yeah . . . I guess."

15

"My mom doesn't go anywhere," Jennifer went on glumly. "She even does the cable shopping network."

Kimberly leaned closer to Buffy. "What did Jeffrey's dad say?"

Buffy lowered her head, doing her best imitation of Jeffrey's father: "'Just remember you're in training, son.'"

"Oh, please." Nicole looked at Kimberly, who rolled her eyes in agreement.

"He is so bald."

The girls began to laugh, but then a voice interrupted them from behind.

"Will you guys shut up, please?"

The girls turned around in their seats.

Two boys were staring at them from a few rows away. One was long and leanly built, with short spiked hair, his black clothes blending into the darkness around him. The other boy was somewhat stockier. His head was shaved, and he wore suspenders. Both of them had on Doc Martens, propped against the seats in front of them.

"It could happen," Buffy answered their question, and was immediately bombarded with popcorn.

"Booo!" the tall one scolded.

"Hiss!" the shorter one chimed in.

"Wrong answer! No prize."

"Gross!" Nicole brushed popcorn off her shoulders. "Take a chill lozenge."

"Like we don't have rights, too?" Kimberly added indignantly.

Buffy turned back toward the screen. "Ignore them."

"I can't believe these people," the short boy said. "We paid money to see this."

The tall one looked at him. "No, we didn't."

"Oh, yeah. But I still want to know what happens."

"Everyone gets horribly killed except the blond girl in the nightie, who finally kills the monster with a machete, but it's not really dead," Buffy said simply.

The boys stared at her.

"You're kidding," Jennifer mumbled. "Is that true?"

"Probably." Buffy shrugged. "What movie is this?"

Outside the theater, a fat yellow moon hovered behind the clouds above the parking lot. The night was still, stirred only by one long howl.

As Jeffrey pulled his BMW convertible into a parking space, Grueller leaned forward in the backseat, wedging his shoulders between Jeffrey and Andy in the front. Tilting back his head, he let out a long, unearthly howl, then laughed as they climbed out and headed toward the theater entrance.

"Look at that moon!" Grueller pointed. "It's huge! Come on, guys, we gotta do something tonight. Party."

"You know," Andy said, "if you'd spend more time at home sleeping, you'd spend less time on the court screwing up."

"You *were* useless out there today." Jeffrey gave Grueller a meaningful glance. "Anyway, I'm booked. Gonna spend some quality time with the little woman."

Andy and Grueller stopped in their tracks, coughing loudly into their hands.

"Wimp! Wimp!"

Jeffrey kept on walking. "You guys are pathetic."

"Later for you, then," Grueller said. "I'm blowing. Andy, you coming?"

"No, I'll hitch a ride with Jeffrey."

"Okay." Grueller shrugged. "Later."

"Head butt!" Andy shouted.

He and Grueller bent over and brought their foreheads together with painstaking slowness, grimacing but barely tapping heads.

"Later," Andy said, laughing, and Grueller headed off through the park.

The theater had begun to empty out now. As

Jeffrey watched for Buffy, he noticed two guys coming out the front door, one in a long black coat, the other with a shaved head. He and Andy stared at them suspiciously, and the guys stared back. Then both pairs began to circle each other, their eyes locked, until the two punkers finally turned and walked away. Before Jeffrey and Andy could follow, the girls appeared, and Buffy went straight into Jeffrey's arms. For a long moment they stood there as if they were the only ones in the whole parking lot, smothering each other with kisses.

"Nice game." Buffy smiled up at Jeffrey.

"Jeffrey, I don't mean to sound sexist or anything," Andy remarked, staring, "but can I *borrow* her?"

"Andy!" Buffy laughed.

"No way," Jeffrey said. "You'd get her dirty." Then, as he saw Buffy's chiding look, "He would, honey. He's an animal."

3

There seemed to be so many shadows tonight.

Grueller walked on and on through the park, until he found himself in a grassy clearing surrounded by trees. He thought he heard something . . . a stealthy, quiet sound . . . and he stopped at once, his ears straining through the night.

Had someone called his name? Or had the bushes just rustled in the breeze?

He looked around hesitantly.

He started forward, then stopped again.

"Yo! Who is that? Don't mess with me, man, I'll rip your head off."

No one answered.

The silence hung around him, heavy and dangerous.

"Come on, come out here," Grueller said, forcing bravado into his voice. "Let's see what you got."

Something stirred . . . whispering . . . hidden . . .

"Forget this," he muttered. He turned on his heel, ready to bolt, but there was someone standing behind him.

Everyone at school knew Wally Bessel. He was a ninth-grade nerd, small for his age and easy to bully, but tonight something seemed different about him. Grueller stared in surprise, taking in Wally's pale, pale face and the strange dead look in his eyes as the kid smiled up at him.

"Bessel! What are you doing here?"

"Hi, Grueller."

"What are you grinning at? You think I was scared?"

"Could be." There was a hollow sound to Wally's voice, as if he was speaking mechanically, not even hearing himself talk. . . .

"You think so?" Grueller said angrily.

"Could be."

Grueller grabbed Wally by the collar and hoisted his small body up in the air. Wally's feet dangled high above the ground.

"Listen, you little worm. I could beat your head to a pulp for you, just like I did last year, you got that? You got that?"

"Got that," Wally repeated tonelessly.

"Good."

And then Wally grabbed Grueller's hands. He grabbed Grueller's hands even as he dangled there, and he began to squeeze them . . . to squeeze them . . . as Grueller's eyes went wide and scared.

"What the . . .?"

Wally smiled even more broadly.

And then he hissed.

He had long fangs, grotesque behind his silver braces.

His head dived at Grueller's neck, lightning quick.

And as Grueller screamed and screamed, the moon slipped free of the clouds and hung there watching.

4

The round, full moon glowed eerily from the TV screen and out into the darkened living room.

Jeffrey sat down on the couch and opened a bag of snacks. He stared for a moment at the original *Dracula* movie on television, then picked up the remote control and clicked to another channel.

". . . the fourth such disappearance in less than two months," a local newscaster announced from his desk. Behind him, a huge photograph of a teenage girl smiled frozenly at the camera. "The sheriff was not available for comment, but a police spokesman issued a statement saying that the situation is not out of hand—"

"We're gonna be late. I knew it."

Jeffrey looked up as Buffy's father went into the kitchen with his suitcase. Buffy was at the microwave making popcorn, and she watched silently as her dad plopped his bag down by the door. Irritated, he wandered out again just as Buffy's mother hurried in with her own luggage, talking to Buffy but not looking at her.

"Now, we'll be back on Sunday, number's on the fridge, don't drive the Jaguar, and tell the maid my underwear does not go in the dishwasher."

Before she had even finished talking, Buffy's mother was hurrying out of the kitchen, and Buffy's father was coming back in.

"Have fun, be good, stay away from the Jag."

Buffy nodded. "I know."

He headed out the door as his wife breezed in again.

"Well, that's everything. Kiss noise."

Her mother made a kiss noise in Buffy's direction, and Buffy stared back at her.

"Bye," Buffy said.

She shook her head slowly as her mom left, then wandered into the living room where Jeffrey was taking everything in.

"Bye-bye, Bobby!" Buffy's mom called out from the front door.

"Bye!" Jeffrey shouted back. He glanced at Buffy. "They think my name's Bobby?"

Buffy began spraying diet butter substitute on her popcorn.

"Well . . . it's possible they think *my* name's Bobby."

"Real 'quality-timers,' huh?"

"Something like that."

"Hey, it works for me." Jeffrey grinned. "If they want to leave you alone in the house, all helpless and vulnerable . . ."

He leaned over to kiss her. Buffy felt his warm, soft breath along her cheek, down her neck. Slyly she sneaked another handful of popcorn into her mouth.

She leaned back by accident onto the remote control, and Dracula reappeared suddenly on the TV screen. Jeffrey immediately became engrossed in the movie.

Staring at the vampire's face, Buffy let her mind drift. After a few minutes, she dozed off to sleep.

It was a filthy place . . . a squalid room in a dark, dingy building. On the bed sat a young Chinese girl wearing hardly any clothes. She had a birthmark on one bare shoulder. A repul-

sive sailor was getting dressed, and as he looked at the girl in disgust, he threw some money down on the bed. The bed was littered with popcorn.

The girl ran out into the hall, but she came hopelessly to a dead end. Standing there waiting for her was a tall figure with smooth, bone-white skin. He smiled at her, and the girl looked up into his face.

The girl was Buffy.

"Soon," Lothos said seductively. "Soon . . ."

"Buffy! Hey, what's the sitch? Wake up!" Jeffrey held her by the shoulders and shook her as she thrashed and moaned.

Gasping, Buffy came to, her eyes slowly focusing on Jeffrey's face.

"Oh, wow," she murmured. "Oh, wow. Oh, wow."

"You were having a nightmare."

Jeffrey settled back, his arms around her, already intent again on the television.

"What'd you dream about?" he asked, almost as an afterthought.

"Nothing."

"Come on, what was it?"

"Nothing," Buffy whispered. "It was just a dream."

5

In a secret place, in a dark and cavernous chamber, torches flickered eerily from walls of hewn rock, throwing macabre patterns of light and shadow deep, deep into fathomless corners. As the shadows crept along the cold stone floor, they licked hungrily at a large, dark pool of blood. The strange hum of an unknown chant throbbed and echoed in the stale, dank air.

An indistinct figure stepped close to the pool and knelt before it. He held his hand over the slimy surface of the blood, and then he leaned forward, separating himself from the shadows around him.

"Sleep, my master, my own," Amilyn hissed, "sleep . . . and feed. I have already begun building you a new family, and soon we will be legion. This place is everything you promised. And when you rise, we will claim it as our own."

He smiled his horrible smile.

"Rubies will drip from your lips," he whispered.

Without warning, a hand shot out of the pool, clamping onto Amilyn's with a terrible strength.

Amilyn leaned over and fervently kissed it.

"Soon . . ." he promised.

6

School hadn't started yet for the day.

As Buffy sat with her usual crowd and waited for the bell to ring, the discussion they'd been having for the last half hour continued in earnest around her.

"The environment," Buffy spoke up.

Jennifer, Nicole, and Kimberly considered this for a moment. Cassandra, another girl who had joined them, looked equally pensive. She was the only one in the group who ever bothered to study, and though she wasn't really their type, they let her hang out with them when they needed something.

"Endangered animals?" Nicole suggested.

Kimberly groaned. "Oh, please."

"Are there any good sicknesses that aren't too depressing?" Jennifer asked.

"Guys. The environment," Buffy persisted. "I'm telling you, it's totally key. The earth is in terrible shape, we could all die, and besides, Sting's doing it."

"I thought he was doing Indians," Kimberly said, looking puzzled.

They all glanced up as Jeffrey and Andy arrived. Jeffrey sat down behind Buffy, and she snuggled back into his arms.

"Hey there." Jeffrey grinned, and Buffy smiled back at him.

"Hi."

"Hi, Jeffrey," Jennifer said shyly.

Andy's eyes swept quickly around the group. "Whatcha guys doing?"

"The senior dance." Nicole tapped her head. "We need to come up with a theme."

"A theme? How about 'the themeless dance'?" Jeffrey said, and laughed.

Andy looked straight at Buffy. "'New dreams, new horizons . . . new boyfriends.' Possible thought . . ."

"Stay away from my girl," Jeffrey growled, teasing, and then to Buffy, "Sorry, honey. 'My woman.'"

"Guys," Kimberly sighed, "try new clue-flakes."

"It has to be, like, a socially conscious theme," Buffy reminded them.

Cassandra nodded seriously and began to read from a memo. "'One that reflects the students' growing awareness of and involvement in the world around them.'"

Jeffrey and Andy groaned in unison. "Downer."

"I still say the environment," Buffy said stubbornly. "That's my suggestion."

"Okay." Kimberly shrugged.

"So, what are the most immediate threats to the world environment right now?" Cassandra asked.

Her pen was poised over her paper, ready to list their opinions. She looked as though she already knew what the answer was, but was waiting to see what they came up with. As she regarded them in total silence, the others looked at each other uncomfortably.

"Well, um . . . litter?" Jeffrey volunteered.

"Litter, yeah!" echoed Andy, beaming.

Everyone but Cassandra was impressed by this.

Jeffrey nodded at her eagerly. "Write that down."

"Okay, what else?" Jennifer prompted.

"Forest fires?" Nicole piped up.

Andy thought out loud. "Communism?"

"Bugs," Buffy said.

Cassandra offered helpfully, "Okay, guys, how about the ozone layer?"

"Oh, yeah!" Kimberly brightened.

"Right!" Nicole echoed.

"We gotta get rid of that!" Buffy agreed. "That's right."

They all looked up as the bell rang and kids started off to class.

"Let's meet tonight, okay?" Kimberly said eagerly. "Café Blasé?"

"Cool." Nicole nodded. "We can figure out decorations and stuff."

Buffy hesitated. "I don't know," she said slowly. "I really want to get a head start on my homework."

There was a long moment of silence.

Everyone stared at Buffy.

Buffy gazed back at her friends, then suddenly burst out laughing, and the others joined in, relieved. The group headed into the school, and Nicole glanced at Buffy, shaking her head in admiration.

"I love that one."

"Yeah," Buffy said proudly, "but you tell it better."

7

Café Blasé was a favorite spot for teenagers to hang out. A faux-fifties diner, it was always bright with lights and noisy with old fifties standards playing on the jukebox. Tonight as Buffy sat with her friends at the end of the counter, she was only vaguely aware of the argument going on around her. Beyond the diner windows, the night seemed uneasy, expectant somehow . . . watchful behind flickering shadows and curling gray mist. . . .

"I don't see why we have to invite everyone," Kimberly said irritably.

"Kimberly," Buffy sighed, forcing her mind

back to the issue at hand, "it's the senior dance."

Nicole nodded in her defense. "If we don't invite all the seniors, we can't use the school funds, you know that."

"Can't they make exceptions?" Kimberly persisted. "Maryanne Heinel? She's *such* a scud. Can't we have a Maryanne clause?"

Nicole straightened up, her eyes on the doorway. "Well, look who's here."

As the girls all turned around, they recognized the two weird guys who'd sat behind them in the movie theater. The pair staggered along the aisle and sat down next to Buffy. Slowly they began pooling their money on the counter, then looked in dismay at the meager result, mostly pennies.

Two dollars and fifty cents.

The tall, lean boy in the long black coat shook his head.

"We're looking at a dog, possible coffee . . ."

Frowning, he shoved his hand into the pocket of his coat and dug deep, finally producing a quarter.

"It's coffee!" he said triumphantly.

"Amazing!" The shorter one nodded his shaved head.

Kimberly leaned in close to her friends.

"Smell much," she remarked, her voice lowered.

"Nice much." Nicole grimaced.

They watched as the tall boy spoke to the waitress.

"Can we have a hot dog, please, medium rare, and a cup of joe?"

Buffy stared at them. "Are you guys for real," she asked, her voice solemn.

"What are you talking to them for?" Jennifer gave Buffy a disapproving look. The short boy also gave Buffy a look, and not a very friendly one.

"What did you say?" he challenged her.

"Yeah, we're for real," the tall one broke in. "We're the real men. What's your name?"

"Buffy."

"Figures," the short one snorted.

"Do people ever call you Buffy the Buffalo?" The tall one seemed amused. "I'm just wondering."

Buffy gave him a withering look.

"They don't," the tall one concluded. "You kind of wish they would, though."

"Wit-tay," Kimberly mumbled.

"I'm sorry," the tall one said, bending forward to see them better. "I'm Pike. This is Benny."

"Pike isn't a name." Kimberly sounded bored. "It's a fish."

The tall boy straightened up. "Hey, wait a minute . . ."

"You're the guys from the movie!" Benny burst out.

"We *hate* you guys!" Pike added good-naturedly.

Together the girls made loud, sarcastic noises as if their hearts were breaking.

"You guys were way rude." Pike shook his head at them. "It was shocking."

"You just snuck in anyway," Nicole fired back.

"So you have to ruin the movie for us? You know, other people have feelings, too."

Kimberly rolled her eyes. "I am so sure."

The waitress brought the hot dog. Benny took it out of the bun, stared at it, then glanced at Buffy.

"Hey, Buffy, what do you think?"

The other girls groaned and turned away in disgust.

Buffy met Benny's eyes.

Her stare was deathly calm.

As her hand closed slowly around the knife beside her plate, Benny gazed back at her, helpless . . . hypnotized . . .

And it seemed to Buffy that the diner began

to fade then, falling away as if it didn't even exist, as if she weren't even there, all the noise and music drifting off, softer and softer into nothingness . . .

Startled, Buffy moved in her seat.

The jukebox was blaring. The diner was bright with chrome and glass and reflections. Customers were talking loudly, and all her friends were looking at her.

Buffy shifted her eyes away from Benny's and let go of her knife.

Benny looked down, shocked.

His hot dog had been sliced off neatly just above his fingers.

"Hey! She wasted my dog!"

Following the direction of Benny's gaze, Pike smiled. "Bummer metaphor."

Nicole was still staring at Buffy, and her voice was slightly awed. "How'd you do that?"

Buffy stared back at her, surprised.

And then she quickly looked away again, rubbing a sudden chill from her arms.

8

Strolling unevenly down the dark street away from the diner, Pike pulled a bottle of mescal from his coat. He took a long swig and handed it over to Benny. The bottle passed back and forth, back and forth, as the friends continued along. They were so busy drinking and talking that they never once noticed the shadowy figure following them in the fog.

"I'll have it running in a week," Pike said, almost wistfully. "It'll be a beauty. It just needs new shocks, you know, brake pads, an engine, and some wheels. It'll be totally cherry."

Benny nodded and gulped deeply from the bottle. "When you get your car together, man, let's bail. Get away from this town, those rich girls. They're a plague, man. They've got to be stopped."

Pike glanced over, deadpan. "You didn't like them."

"They're all the same! They're so stuck up, they're just . . . they're not even human. I hate them."

"Would you go out with them?"

"Yes. Definitely. Definitely. Please, God."

"Well, there it is, isn't it?" Pike said philosophically. "You don't even like them, and you'd go out with them. What's that all about?"

"I got a news flash, man—another shot of this, and I'll even go out with *you.*"

"Oh, yeah, and then you'll never call me."

They came to the edge of a steep incline overlooking the valley below. A waist-high concrete wall rose out of the earth, and the boys stood there for a moment beneath a huge tree, both of them peering off into the quiet night.

Pike finished the mescal, ate the worm, and chucked the bottle over the wall. A long moment passed before they heard the shattering of glass.

Benny wavered and caught hold of his friend.

"I think I'm gonna ralf."

Leaning over the wall, he hung his head down while Pike nodded at him in total sympathy.

"Don't worry, Benny. I'm here for you."

Pike promptly fell over backward.

"I'm here for you, Ralf," he managed to mumble again just before he passed out.

Still waiting to get sick, Benny didn't notice that Pike was out cold. Nor did he notice the shadowy figure slowly approaching him from behind . . . the figure that was only a few feet away from him now.

Without warning, a hand shot down from nowhere and grabbed Benny's face.

Benny didn't even have time to react.

In one split second of shock, he felt himself being heaved upward, saw the hideous face looking straight at him from a low branch of the tree. He saw the motorcycle jacket—the sunglasses—the punked-out hair. And he saw the grin. The horrible, fiendish, hungry grin . . .

"You wanna go for a ride?" Amilyn hissed.

And then they were falling, on and on and on . . . out of the tree . . . past the wall . . . just as the shadowy figure reached it at last.

The man in the shabby black clothes ran to the wall and looked over, but the two were already lost in the dark, swirling mist below.

Slowly the man turned and looked about. He dug in his pockets and pulled out a cross and a stake. He drew out an old, stained picture and laid it on the railing. And then, with the stake and cross held tightly in his hand, he stood beside Pike and gazed pensively into the deep, endless night.

The picture was of a ten-year-old girl about to blow out the candles on her birthday cake.

The cake read: Happy Birthday, Buffy.

9

Hey, I was thinking," Jennifer said breathlessly, sitting down on the gym floor after she finished a back flip. "For the dance, what about a big sign that says Don't Tread on Me. You know, and a picture of the earth."

The other girls paused from their after-school practice session and looked at each other.

"Don't tread on the earth?" Buffy looked dismayed.

Nicole shook her head and bent to tie her shoe. "I don't get it."

"How do you not tread on the earth?" Buffy went on. "I mean, you kind of have to."

"I never thought of that," Jennifer agreed.

"I gotta bail." Nicole glanced around the deserted gym and then back at Buffy. "You coming?"

"You guys blow." Buffy waved them off. "I'm waiting on Cassandra. She's gonna help me with my history."

"Cassandra's really smart." Nicole stared at her, and Buffy shrugged.

"Yeah . . . she's okay, though."

Nicole gave her a funny look. "I guess."

"Are you going out with Jeffrey tonight?" Jennifer asked casually.

"Jealous?" Buffy teased, and heard her friend's uncomfortable laugh. "Don't worry, Jennifer. Someday your prince will come."

Nicole grinned. "Yeah, just make sure you catch him."

The other girls left, the sound of their footsteps fading eerily out the door. Buffy looked around at the empty bleachers, the empty court. Tentatively, she started doing a routine. Then, as her adrenaline pumped up, she ran toward the middle of the court and jumped, flying into an amazing series of gymnastic flips and cartwheels. Rolling through one final aerial somersault, she landed perfectly on her feet and looked up.

The man was standing right in front of her, only inches away.

He wore black, shabby clothes, like a rumpled priest. . . .

Buffy screamed and jumped back.

"Where did you come from? You scared me to death!"

"I'm sorry," he said politely. "That was impressive. The . . . tumbling."

His accent was formal and clipped, very British.

"What?" Buffy stared at him, her fear fading now, easing into bewilderment. "Oh. I used to do gymnastics. Are you looking for someone?"

"I'm looking for you, actually."

"Am I in trouble or something?"

"Not at all. My name is Merrick. I was sent to find you some time ago. I should have found you much sooner, but there were . . . complications. You should have been taught, prepared."

Buffy narrowed her eyes. "What are you talking about?"

"I've searched the entire world for you, Buffy."

"Why?"

"To bring you . . . your birthright."

"My birthright?" Her expression was more

confused than ever. "You mean, like a trust fund?"

Merrick only stared at her.

"I had a trust fund from my great-grandfather," Buffy mused, thinking back, "or maybe it was an inheritance, 'cause he's dead, and I spent it on shoes."

"You must come with me," Merrick said calmly. "It's much too late already. You must come with me to the graveyard."

"Wait a minute. My birthright is in the graveyard? Later *not.*"

"Wait!"

"You're one of those dirty old men that, like, attack girls and stuff," Buffy declared, stiffening indignantly. "Forget you. My, um, boyfriend is gonna be here in about thirty seconds, and he's *way* testy."

"You don't understand," Merrick tried to explain. "You have been chosen."

"Chosen to go to the graveyard? Why don't you just take the first runner-up, okay?"

"You must believe me. You must come with me while there's still time."

"Time to do what?"

"To stop the killing," Merrick said flatly. "To stop the vampires."

Buffy's mouth opened in surprise. She regarded him for a long, long moment.

"Let me get this straight. You're, like, this greasy bum, and I have to go to the graveyard with you 'cause I'm chosen, and there's vampires."

"Yes."

"Does Elvis talk to you? Tell you to do things? Do you see spots?"

"I don't have time for your prattling," Merrick broke in, almost irritably. "I have proof. You bear the mark."

Before she could answer, he stepped forward and pulled the neck of her shirt aside, revealing her shoulder.

"The mark of the Order!" he exclaimed. "The—where's the mark?"

There was no birthmark on Buffy's shoulder.

Flustered, Merrick looked at her other one.

"The mark of the—wait a minute."

Annoyed, Buffy shoved his hand away.

"You mean that big hairy mole? Excuse me: eeyuu. I had it removed. And, like, knowing about my big old mole isn't proof of anything except that it's way past medication time. Just stay away from me, okay?"

She started to walk away.

"Did you ever dream that you were someone else?" he asked.

Buffy froze. A strange look flickered across her face. She didn't speak at first, but when she did, her voice was cautious.

"Everybody does."

"In the past," Merrick insisted. "A girl. Maybe . . . a Magyar peasant. An Indian princess. A slave."

Slowly, slowly, Buffy turned back to face him.

"I was a slave."

"In Virginia." Merrick nodded.

"I don't know. It was . . . there was a big farm or something. And there's one, I'm in this dark, dirty room . . ."

"China."

"Oh, wow. I never told anybody about this." Buffy's voice grew thin and excited. "I remember the one about the peasant, too. I mean, there's a bunch. Is this, like, channeling or something?"

Merrick rolled his eyes, and Buffy rushed on.

"I had a dream once where I was . . . there were, like, knights in it, and I worked in this tavern. And I was fighting. I'm always fighting. And there's a guy . . . he's not always there, but he's horrible, all white, and he's always . . . trying to kill me."

"Lothos."

Buffy flinched. A cold, slow tremor went up her spine.

"How do you know all this?"

"I have to show you," Merrick said.

10

The sun began to slip down, thick and orange, beyond the hills.

As Merrick led Buffy through the graveyard, long black fingers of shadow oozed over the ground, as if trying to point the way to the one particular grave they were seeking.

"I can't believe I'm doing this," Buffy mumbled, following Merrick through the crouching maze of headstones. "I can't believe I'm in a graveyard with a strange man hunting for vampires on a school night."

"Why didn't you ever tell anybody about your dreams?" Merrick asked curiously.

"Oh, yeah, tell everyone I'm crazy. Beauty

idea." She paused and gave a slight wince. "Ow."

"Feeling a little pain?" Merrick looked at her intently, knowingly.

"None of your business. You're so nosy."

"This is it."

Abruptly Buffy stopped, only to realize she was standing on a freshly dug grave. Leaning down, she squinted through the gloom to read the headstone:

ROBERT BERMAN
1972–1990
GOD IS AT HIS HEELS

"Robert Berman was killed three days ago." Merrick's voice echoed ghostly in the heavy silence of the dead. "The body was found in the bushes out by the canal. Extensive tissue damage—tearing—at the neck and shoulders. Coroner thinks it was a dog. You sit here."

He pointed to a plot of ground about eight feet from the end of the grave. Buffy sat and leaned against another stone marker, watching as Merrick reached into his jacket. To her surprise, he pulled out a stake and a cross, then handed the cross to her.

"Wait a minute—" Buffy started to get up, but Merrick's touch was reassuring.

"Just for protection. You won't have to do anything. I just need you to watch."

"All right. What do we do now?"

"We wait for Robert to wake up."

Merrick went over to the dead boy's headstone and crouched beside it.

"Do you have any gum?" Buffy asked nervously.

She looked around at the thickening shadows just as the last red glimmer of sun disappeared behind the hills.

Darkness had settled over the school.

As Cassandra stood waiting for Buffy, she checked her watch again and frowned. The schoolyard had been deserted for a long time now, but just to make certain, she let her eyes make one last thorough sweep of the area.

Buffy must have forgotten, she decided. I might as well go home . . .

She headed across the empty parking lot toward her car. Taking her key out of her purse, she slipped it into the lock on her door.

And then she stopped.

Something rustled behind her, very softly . . .

Slowly Cassandra turned around.

11

Buffy fidgeted.

Nothing seemed real to her anymore—none of this graveyard business, this vampire nonsense, this silly old man crouching there in position beside the headstone.

She played with her fingernails and watched as Merrick tilted his head and listened.

And then she heard it, too.

A low moan, trembling under the ground. . . .

Buffy sat up straight, holding the cross to her. The moan became louder . . . louder . . . until it was almost a scream.

But the next sound was the worst of all.

Fingers scraping wood—wood splintering —something digging, clawing its way out . . .

Buffy looked at Merrick, stunned.

They didn't have long to wait.

As fingers suddenly broke through the ground, the moan became a triumphant hiss. For an interminable second, the hand held itself stiff in the open air, and then the fingers bent and clutched at the earth.

Robert Berman burst halfway out of his grave like a macabre jack-in-the-box, his face filthy and dead white. As he spotted Buffy in front of him, he bobbed toward her with a crazed grin, stretching and straining for her neck.

Merrick dropped down behind Robert and grabbed him. Through a haze of terror, Buffy saw Merrick raise the stake, but she couldn't seem to move.

Without warning, a pair of arms shot up through the grave right below Buffy. Horrified, she felt rotting hands clamp ruthlessly onto her and drag her down. As she struggled to lift her head from the ground, the vampire face of a young woman emerged next to her, grinning at her from the crumbling earth. Buffy shrieked and fought to break away.

Merrick looked up, momentarily distracted by Buffy's screams, and Robert saw his chance. Furiously, he threw Merrick off and pulled himself swiftly out of the grave. As Merrick fell to the ground, the stake went flying.

Buffy wrenched out of the woman's grasp, scrambled to her feet, and started to run. As she felt the woman grab her again, she suddenly remembered the cross in her hand. Spinning around, she thrust it against the vampire's forehead. There was a horrible sizzling sound and the smell of burnt flesh, and then the creature fell to the ground, screaming in agony.

"Bye, now," Buffy said breathlessly, and again she took off.

Several feet away, Merrick and Robert were still struggling. Robert lifted Merrick by the shoulders, his lips drawing back in a sneer, and he prepared to bite.

A stake exploded through the front of his chest, driven clear through from his back.

He fell forward with a look of shocked disbelief. Buffy stood behind him and watched him die.

"Where's the other one?" Merrick asked urgently, picking himself up off the ground.

"She—"

Before Buffy could finish, the woman leaped at her, shrieking in rage. Twisting violently, Buffy managed to disentangle herself as Merrick produced yet another stake and threw it to her.

Buffy didn't even hesitate. She rammed the stake straight through the vampire's heart.

The woman gave one final scream, her repulsive face still smoking even as she died.

Several drops of blood spattered onto Buffy's sweater.

For a long, silent moment Buffy looked down at herself . . . down at the stains of dark, red blood.

She didn't remember going home.

She didn't remember anything else until she finally looked up again to find herself outside her own front door.

She glanced around, dazed, trying to follow the sound of Merrick's voice.

"Go to school tomorrow," he was instructing her. "Try to act normal. Don't let anyone know what's happening. This is important. When the vampires find out who you are . . . *you* won't be hunting *them* anymore."

Buffy walked the last few feet up to the house. She was slow and mechanical, like a sleepwalker caught in a dream.

"All right," she murmured.

Merrick handed her a piece of paper. "Meet me at this address after school."

"I have cheerleading squad," she said tonelessly.

"Skip it."

Buffy nodded. Merrick started back down the walkway.

"Merrick?" Buffy said suddenly.

Merrick stopped, waited.

"They can't come in, right? Unless you invite them. Is that true?"

"It's true."

Buffy watched as Merrick disappeared into the night. Then she went into the house.

She shut the door and turned to go upstairs. Someone was standing behind her, and she recoiled, swallowing a scream.

"Do you know what time it is?" Buffy's mother demanded, clamping her hands on her hips as she glared at her daughter.

Buffy could only guess what she must look like after her graveyard confrontation, and she stood there uncomfortably, not knowing what to say.

"Ummm . . . around ten?" she ventured innocently.

Her mother tapped her watch, looking even more annoyed.

"I *knew* this thing was slow."

As Buffy stared, not believing her luck, her mother went off into the next room.

"You pay a fortune for something," she muttered, and then shouted, "Honey, come on, we're gonna be late!"

Buffy let out a long sigh and went up to her room.

She couldn't stop thinking about what had happened.

She stood at the bathroom sink for a long time, trying to scrub the blood off her shirt. She wanted desperately to cry, but she kept holding back her tears.

Ready for bed at last, she sat in the middle of the bed with her blankets pooled around her. She couldn't sleep. She couldn't do anything but remember Merrick and the vampires and everything else that should have been impossible. . . .

Finally, exhausted, she lay back on her pillow.

And then she closed her eyes.

12

Buffy had no idea if she'd really slept at all. Her night had been filled with troubled images that had kept her tossing on the very edge of consciousness, and when morning had finally come, she'd awoken sweaty and exhausted.

Now, as she walked slowly through the halls at school, she saw Gary Murray, the school counselor, come up beside her and glance pointedly at his watch. That could only mean she was late for class, but right now she didn't care. She continued on dazedly through the building, and met Jeffrey going the other way.

"Hey, baby, how ya doing?" Jeffrey stopped beside her. "You look beat."

"I do?" Buffy said. "I guess I do."

"Where were you last night? I called your house, like, four times."

"I went to sleep. I think I have the flu or something."

Jeffrey backed away from her.

"I can't get sick. You know—training and all. I'm gonna be late."

"Bye."

Jeffrey hurried off to class. Buffy walked on a little farther and bumped into Nicole.

"Hey, Buffers. You look thrashed."

"Thanks."

"You and Cassandra get anything done last night?"

Buffy looked confused for a moment. It was such an effort to think, to make herself remember.

"Oh. No." Buffy shook her head. "She never showed."

Cassandra opened her eyes.

Her head was splitting, and as she struggled to sit up, fresh pain washed through her head, making her dizzy.

She blinked a few times and looked around.

She was lying on a floor of cold stone, and rock walls rose high on every side. Torchlight flickered over her face, illuminating a pool close beside her that seemed to be filled with dark, dark water.

She tried to get up, but couldn't. She managed to pull herself over to the pool, and then she splashed water on her face.

Only it wasn't water that ran down her cheeks and trickled into the corners of her mouth, that suddenly filled her senses with a warm, metallic sweetness . . .

It was blood.

In slow, growing horror, Cassandra stared at her hands, at the thick red liquid running down her wrists, onto her clothes, making puddles around her on the cold, cold floor.

She didn't see the figure at first, rising from the pool, his bare chest, his old-fashioned trousers and boots, . . .

His bone-white face.

Not a drop of blood seemed to touch Lothos as he rose.

He looked at Cassandra, his lazy eyes going from her head to her feet.

"I find it restorative, sleeping in the life-blood of so many," he said matter-of-factly, "to feel their souls coursing about me."

Cassandra pulled back, dragging herself away from him across the floor. "What's happening! What do you want!"

Lothos smiled. "So very much."

"My parents have money—"

"Yes, I'm sure they do. This place is everything you said it was, Amilyn."

Cassandra spun around. Amilyn stood behind her, grinning, and as she recoiled in terror, he hissed and bared his fangs.

"What . . . are you?" she stammered.

"Are we so strange?" Lothos said easily. "So alien to you? I've seen this culture, the wealth, the greed, the waste . . . it's truly heartwarming. The perfect place to spread my empire. Honestly"—he paused for a moment, thinking—"Eastern Europe was so dead, the Communists just drained the blood out of the place. Took me seventy years just to get a visa." Again he smiled. "It's livened up a bit in the past few years, but it's nothing compared to this . . . this Mecca of consumption. The City of Angels."

Again Cassandra tried to move away from him, but he was beside her immediately, as if she hadn't moved at all.

"What are we?" He considered. "We are man perfected. We exist to consume."

In the shadows, Amilyn mouthed the words along with Lothos, his eyes turned to the ceiling, as if he'd heard the speech a hundred times before.

Cassandra fumbled frantically in her purse. She pulled a plastic credit card out of her wallet.

"Here, look. My gold card. It's yours. I'll never report it."

Amilyn snatched it from her and looked it over.

"What do you say?" Lothos said smoothly. "Do we change this one, or do we just kill her?"

Amilyn bit into the card. "I don't think this one is gold."

"Listen," Cassandra babbled desperately, "you don't want me. You want bodies, I'll help you. I mean it. I won't say a word. I swear to God—"

Lothos grabbed her so swiftly and suddenly that she didn't even have time to gasp before he broke her neck.

"I wish you wouldn't mention Him," Lothos sighed, profoundly annoyed.

Slowly Cassandra slid down the wall, her eyes fixed and glazed over.

Behind her, stenciled onto the stone, a few

faded words glimmered softly in the glow of
the torches:

HEMERY HIGH SCHOOL
MAINTENANCE ONLY

13

The other girls were already suited up for cheerleading practice when Buffy wandered into the dressing room. She put her bag down on the floor next to her locker and looked around listlessly, as if wondering how she'd gotten there.

"I didn't think you'd show today," Nicole said, studying Buffy with a puzzled frown.

"No, I'm gonna practice," Buffy mumbled.

"Cool. See you out there."

The girls left Buffy to undress. As she started to unbutton her jeans, she suddenly spotted Merrick standing at the end of the lockers, staring at her. Startled, she jumped back.

"What are you doing here? This a naked place."

"You were supposed to be at the warehouse half an hour ago," Merrick said evenly.

"I told you, I have practice."

"And I told you—"

"Look," Buffy broke in, her voice strained, "I think there's been a big mistake here. I mean, I appreciate that there's real vampires, and you have this big holy mission and all that, but somewhere along the way someone read their tea leaves wrong, 'cause I ain't your girl. You know? I think there's a girl with big manly muscles and maybe a yucky girl-mustache who's just waiting for someone like you. I don't think I'm up to this, and just between us"—she gave him a meaningful look— "neither do you."

Merrick was silent for a moment, letting Buffy's speech sink in.

"It's true," he conceded at last, "you're not what I expected."

"See?"

"Certainly you're unprepared—"

"Don't I know it."

"Untrained, clumsy, without a doubt the most vacuous candidate in my entire—"

"Okay," Buffy cut him off irritably, "I think we both get the point."

Merrick nodded. "I guess there's nothing more for us to talk about."

"I guess not." Buffy stood there for a moment watching as Merrick headed toward the door. "Good luck and all," she added lamely.

Merrick turned back to look at her.

"Oh. There is one thing."

"Yeah?"

With lightning speed, Merrick hurled a knife straight at her head. Before Buffy even had time to blink, she had already caught the weapon, only inches from her face.

Buffy froze, eyes fixed on the knife in her hand.

And then she burst into tears.

"You threw a knife at my head!"

It was a reaction Merrick hadn't expected, and it took him a second to answer.

"I had to test you," he tried to explain.

"But you threw a knife at my head!"

"And you caught it!" he insisted cheerfully. "Only the chosen one could have done that."

"Don't you get it?" Buffy wailed. "I don't *want* to be the chosen one! I don't *want* to spend the rest of my life chasing after vampires! I just want to graduate from high school, go to Europe, marry Christian Slater, and *die*. It may not sound too exciting to a sconehead like you, but I think it's swell. And then you come along . . . and . . . and then I'm a member of the hairy mole club, so you throw things at me!"

As Merrick watched in dismay, Buffy seemed to exercise every ounce of control to pull herself together. And then, slowly and deliberately, she began coming at him, her eyes blazing with anger.

Merrick began to back up.

"It was necessary." He held out his hands, trying to soothe her, but Buffy was beyond being comforted.

"Last night," she said furiously, a slow awareness growing in her eyes, "you knew I was sitting on a fresh grave, didn't you?"

Merrick took another step away, shaking his head. "I don't think you understand the full implications of—"

Buffy punched him in the face. He went flying several feet, then landed on his back, his nose bleeding profusely.

Buffy stopped and looked down at him, her mouth dropping open.

"Wow . . ."

The warehouse was gray and old and dusty, long since abandoned. Despite the layers of grime that caked its large windows, sunlight still managed to seep in, probing the shadows,

revealing stacks of wooden crates and manne-
quin body parts scattered here and there,
leaning and lying in macabre positions.

Buffy followed Merrick through the hazy
light, chattering as she glanced around at her
surroundings.

"I'll tell you the truth. I never hit anyone
before."

Merrick glanced over at her quickly. He was
still holding a rag to his bloody nose, and now
he tried to speak through it. "You're priddy
good ad it."

"My hand doesn't even hurt."

"I'b so glad."

He pulled the rag away, folded it up, and put
it in his pocket, gingerly touching his tender
nose.

"You shouldn't underestimate yourself,"
Merrick scolded her gently. "You've got pow-
ers you've only just begun to tap. Physical,
mental prowess you've never dreamed of. I've
administered a few shocks to your system to
start the adrenaline working. I'm sorry I have
to take so many shortcuts in the training
process."

As he spoke, Buffy continued to look around
at the dim warehouse and its contents. She ran
one finger slowly along the top of a crate, then

gazed down at the thick film of dust she'd acquired.

"Am I the only one?" she asked quietly.

"What?"

"The only Slayer. Are there more? Do they have support groups or anything?"

"There are girls," Merrick informed her, "all over the world, who are different. Who have the potential to become Slayers. But only one is chosen."

"I get it. It's just like winning the lottery, only it stinks." Buffy sat down on a crate and looked back at him. "How come I got the winning ticket?"

Merrick hesitated. "Do you know what a Vampire-King is?"

"I don't know. You mean, like Dracula?"

"He is one, yes." Merrick nodded. "Well, when the signs foretell a Slayer's ascendance—"

He broke off, seeing by her expression that she didn't have the slightest idea what he was talking about. He took a deep breath and started again.

"When we pick a lucky winner, it's usually because there is a Vampire-King nearby. From his prevalence in your dreams, I'd say it was Lothos."

"Swell."

"See, Vampire-Kings move about, usually with one or two of their followers to lay the groundwork. They find a community, feed on it, make it their own. Usually this goads the community into a kind of paranoid frenzy, but for some reason, nobody here seems to be paying any attention. But the only ones who can face the Kings, the ones—"

He stopped again, noticing that Buffy had raised her hand.

"What is it?"

"Do I have to take notes on this?" Buffy frowned.

14

It didn't take Buffy long to realize what she was in for: Cheerleading practice was *nothing* compared to training sessions with Merrick.

It was a slow process—often painful. While Amilyn and his vampire cohorts went about stealing and killing and generally terrorizing the city night after night, Buffy and Merrick secluded themselves in the warehouse, working out their battle plans. More than ever now, Buffy felt the need to keep herself in top physical condition. She did endless gymnastic routines while Merrick sat nearby on a crate, reading obituaries and circling certain entries.

And Buffy could tell from the scowl on his face that they were running out of time.

Being late for school was becoming a habit. Every morning now Gary Murray watched Buffy trailing along the hallway, and she knew he kept a careful record of her tardiness.

She was more distracted than ever. She recognized the hurt on Jeffrey's face when she was so anxious to leave him after school, and, guiltily, she would give him a long, lingering kiss, wishing she could tell him what was happening, still not totally understanding it herself.

Sometimes she and Merrick played computer games during the afternoons, like Gameboy and Super Mario Brothers. Merrick would grow more and more frustrated, at the mercy of the game, and struggle for all he was worth, only to die in the end.

"Ooh, another embarrassment for the tea bag, while the chosen one is close to an all-time record," Buffy would tease him, mimicking the voice of an announcer, and then laugh at Merrick's indignation.

"I don't believe this game is really helpful," Merrick would complain.

"It teaches strategy," she assured him.

"Strategy? I died from stepping on a turtle."

Buffy would take the game from him and

start her own turn, and then questions would pop into her mind.

"Were there ever any, like, famous vampires?"

"Absolutely. You've heard of the emperor Caligula, perhaps? Or Jack the Ripper?"

"They were vampires?"

"Same one."

"Oh."

And she would consider this for a moment, looking at Merrick. And then her player, also, would die.

"Hey!"

Seeing her worry, Merrick would reach for the game again, but she'd peevishly hold onto it. They'd glare at each other like spoiled children, tugging at their toy, and for the moment the magnitude of their mission would be forgotten.

Merrick never let up. Even when Buffy felt like dropping from exhaustion, he made her work. He would spar with her, working back and forth, in and out between the crates. He knew Buffy was his superior in speed and strength, yet he could still trip her easily, and she grew more determined than ever to beat him each time she glared up at him from the floor.

Yet often Buffy came up with clever tactics

of her own, things that both surprised and amused Merrick, while causing him at the same time to roll his eyes heavenward and ask for strength. It had been entirely Buffy's idea to go into a church one afternoon and find a priest.

"Excuse me . . ." she said, approaching hesitantly, as the priest turned with a beneficent smile.

"Yes, my child? Is something troubling you?"

"Well, sort of." Buffy bit her lip, and the priest nodded encouragingly.

"Well, maybe I can help."

"Yeah. Um . . . could you bless these?"

Buffy held up a six-pack of Perrier.

15

Lothos sat in his secret place.

Sallow torchlight sputtered across the dark surface of the pool, and the air was thick with the odor of warm, rich blood.

He held a dead girl in his arms. Her body was draped gracefully across his lap.

To an innocent onlooker, it could almost have been a beautiful scene, a romantic and poetic scene, reminiscent of Michelangelo's *Pieta.*

Lothos sat perfectly still.

His eyes were calm, hazy with a faraway look.

And then, in the deep, deep silence . . . he belched.

16

Buffy's grueling education continued.

Hour after hour she sat in the warehouse listening to Merrick's lectures and explanations, wondering when it would all end, wondering how she could possibly remember it all. Sometimes she grew so weary that she'd sit staring at her mentor, staring but not really seeing him, not even really hearing him anymore, just doodling in her notebook and nodding from time to time in a mechanical way.

Merrick wasn't fooled.

"Lothos was probably born in the eleventh or twelfth century," Merrick sermonized one afternoon. "He's been difficult to trace. His power has increased with age. It will be a long while before you are ready to face him." The old man sighed. "We'll be lucky if we can get him to leave the area, to lie low for a while. That will scatter the rest of them. Lothos is . . ."

His voice trailed off as he looked down at Buffy. She hadn't acknowledged him for some time and was staring raptly at her notebook.

". . . is extremely powerful," Merrick went on slowly, "but he is still a vampire, and vulnerable to the same . . ."

Merrick narrowed his eyes and leaned closer to her. He wondered if she had heard anything he'd said in the last half hour.

"Daylight is still his enemy. The stake can still find his heart."

He glared at Buffy. No response.

"I have huge antlers growing out of my nose," Merrick said.

"Uh-huh," Buffy mumbled.

Merrick slammed a stake right through the middle of her notebook. With a scream, Buffy jumped backward and landed hard, sitting on the floor.

"WHAT!" she exclaimed furiously.

"Try to pay attention," Merrick ordered, and went back to his lecture.

It seemed Merrick never ran out of things he thought she should know.

When the afternoon sessions dragged long into the nights, Buffy drank cup after cup of coffee and tried to stay awake. She didn't even realize how worn out she was until the day in class when Nicole tried to cheat off her during a test, and Buffy slumped and fell over, fast asleep.

She supposed it was inevitable that she would end up in Gary Murray's office sooner or later.

Sagging tiredly in a chair, Buffy watched as Gary moved about his desk, sitting behind it, leaning on it, trying to carry on an amicable conversation. She could hardly concentrate on what he was saying, but for some strange reason, she was acutely aware of a fly that was buzzing around Gary's head.

"Well, I think we can safely say that something's going on with you, Buffy," Gary said in his friendliest manner. "Now, there's nothing to be nervous about; you're not in any trouble. Don't think of me as Gary Murray, administrator. Think of me as Gary Murray, party guy! Happening dude who can talk to the young. Tell me." He leaned forward conspiratorially. "It's stress, isn't it?"

Buffy saw his lips moving, but suddenly her mind was out of the office and faraway.

She was thinking about the mall . . . how she'd gone there recently with Nicole and Jennifer and Kimberly, and how, suddenly, she had seemed so different from the rest of them. . . .

Her mind shifted, wavering between her memory and Gary Murray's office. The fly was buzzing again, louder and louder in her brain. . . .

She had been at the mall in her cool, funky clothes and very little makeup, and when she'd caught a glimpse of her reflection in a store window, it had hit her for the very first time how very different she was now from her friends. She had seen the empty extra holes in her earlobes and the dark roots showing in her hair because she wasn't dying it blond anymore. She had stood there listening to Nicole and Jennifer and Kimberly talking, and she'd realized how much more comfortable she felt with herself these days, how much more confident and self-possessed.

She and her friends had stopped to look at some dresses, and something in the next store had caught Buffy's eye, making her stare and stare until she had finally wandered off again. . . .

A chainsaw poster. . . .

The fly buzzed annoyingly, startling Buffy once more from her reverie.

She was still in Gary Murray's office, staring at him expressionlessly as he rambled on and on and the fly kept humming. Buffy reached over to the table beside her and picked up a pushpin.

"Hey, I know where you're coming from." Gary shrugged sympathetically. "Believe me, I've done it all. Had some real experiences in the sixties. Well, the late seventies, too, actually. I was a real wild man."

Buffy slyly sneaked the pushpin into her mouth.

"Oh, I'm not proud of it, looking back," Gary went on.

He was leaning over his desk now, looking right at her, and the fly was buzzing louder and louder and louder. . . .

"Sure, I made mistakes and I thought I was cool"—Gary shook his head ruefully—"and I thought, Hey, I know all there is to know about life. I don't need any advice from that other generation. What did they know about anything . . ."

Buffy watched Gary. As he glanced away for a second, she spit out the pushpin.

The buzzing stopped.

* * *

In the warehouse that night with Merrick, Buffy sparred with renewed strength, maneuvering expertly around the crates with a stake clutched tightly in her hand.

This time she pinned him.

As Buffy looked down at Merrick, she aimed the stake at his solar plexus.

Merrick gazed back at her.

Slowly he moved the point above his heart.

CUT.... THE THIRD STRIKE

In the waterlogged dim light, with Mahoney

Once she phoned the

17

Pike lay across his bed as the Posies blasted "Help Yourself" from his stereo system. His room was in a total shambles, a state he considered comfortable and which didn't bother him in the least. Outside his first-floor window, the night stretched out, endless and still.

He didn't see the sudden stirring of the darkness . . .

Or the figure creeping slowly toward his house.

Benny pressed close to the window, trying to peer into the room. His face was as familiar as always, yet there was something frighteningly

different about it tonight, tainting his features
with a look of the dead. He scraped his fingers
across the glass, and called out softly.

"Pike . . ."

Pike sat up and turned down the music. He
looked around the room, then went to the
window and tried to open it.

It was stuck.

"Benny, man, where you been? You bailed
on me—I passed out, man, I almost did a Jimi
Hendrix!"

"Let me in," Benny said.

Pike struggled with the window and kept on
talking.

"This weird English guy gave me a ride
home—I thought he was gonna hit on me,
but—"

He broke off then, getting a good look at
Benny for the first time. He stood there and
stared.

"Invite me in, Pike." Benny's voice was
eager, but Pike didn't move.

"Wait a minute. What's wrong with you,
man?"

"I'm fine."

"You look awful, Benny."

Benny grinned, and pressed his slimy forehead against the glass.

"I . . . feel . . . pretty."

"No offense, man, but I think you're on something nasty." Pike frowned. "Why don't you just go and cool out, and I'll see you in the morning or something."

"The sun!" Benny cried. "It burns! It BURNS!"

He laughed at his impression, and brown spittle flew out of his mouth, coating the windowpane.

"Let me in, Pike! I'm hungry!"

"Get away from here."

"I'm hungry."

"I mean it."

Pike backed slowly away from the window.

18

The street was swallowed in blackness . . . silent and deserted.

Buffy walked slowly through the dark, trying to appear nonchalant, yet her eyes darted constantly from side to side, probing the thick, murky shadows.

"Sure is cold. What a dark night. Nice night for a walk."

She began to whistle, and then, after a few more steps, she began to sing.

"'Feelings, la la la la, feelings . . . ' Boy, I'm helpless."

As she passed an alleyway, she heard a soft

rustling amid the garbage cans. Cautiously she moved toward the noise. The shadows thickened around her, distorted and deceptive. About halfway down the alley, a rat suddenly scurried away from the cans and disappeared down a drain.

"Yeucch."

And then Buffy heard another sound . . .

Behind her.

With painstaking slowness, she turned to face the vampire standing at the alleyway entrance.

They stared at each other, some thirty feet apart.

"Hello . . ." Buffy said softly.

She moved back a step.

The vampire advanced one.

"What do you want?"

Hissing, the creature charged. Buffy looked around frantically and realized she was trapped.

The vampire struck her at top speed, and she instantly rolled onto her back, flipping the creature and hurling it against the wall at the end of the alley. As the vampire hit, Buffy, still rolling, snatched a stake from inside her jacket and threw it directly at the vampire's heart. The stake barely punctured its chest, but before the creature could move, Buffy threw a roundhouse kick, driving the stake all the way home with her foot.

The vampire screamed and sank to the ground.

Buffy turned triumphantly.

"Toaster-caked him!"

And then she waited while Merrick clicked his stopwatch and stepped into the alley and looked at her.

Merrick parked his old Dodge Dart near the warehouse.

It was the same routine they'd been through many times before—talking as they walked to the door, Buffy keeping an eye out for trouble while Merrick got the lock open.

"He was slow," Merrick told her. "Very simple. They won't all be that easy."

"Fine."

"And the alley was a mistake. Never corner yourself like that. If they'd come at you in force, you'd be dead now. One vampire is a lot easier to kill than ten."

"Does the word 'duhh' mean anything to you?"

Merrick regarded her for a moment. "You felt a little sick, didn't you? The cramps."

They entered the warehouse and began to unload their supplies, even as they argued.

"Nice conversationalist!" Buffy retorted. "Yeah, I felt 'em a little, *since* you're so excited about the subject."

"It's natural," Merrick said blandly. "A reaction to their presence, to the . . . unnaturalness of it. It's part of how you are able to track them."

"Oh, *wonderful*. That's just great. Thanks for telling me."

"You'll get used to it. I'm more worried about your tactical mistake."

"You are such a wet," Buffy muttered.

"A what?"

"A wet! Didn't I just kill that vampire? I think I did. I didn't see you killing any vampires. You were too busy playing beat the clock."

"Don't start with me again," Merrick warned.

"Aren't I, like, the chosen one? The one and only? The Grand High Poobah, and doesn't that mean you have to be nice to me? Like, *ever?*"

"Buffy—"

"And why do you always wear black? It's so down. It's totally not your color. I don't think you have a color."

"What do you want? Encouragement?" Merrick went on in a bad American accent: "Gosh, Buffy, you're so special, I just want to give you a great big hug, oh, I'm just having a warm fuzzy."

"Oh, why don't you just leave me alone!"

Merrick turned on her in carefully controlled anger.

"Do you know how many girls I've trained to be Slayers? *Five*. Five properly prepared girls, girls who faced their responsibilities, who worked hard to become women overnight —harder than you've ever worked in your life—and I saw them ripped apart. Do you want to live? *Do* you?"

"I—"

"What did you think, that being able to jump about and hit people makes you a Slayer?"

Buffy stared at him for a long, silent moment.

"Five?" she finally echoed.

"Five."

"So, basically, I've got the life expectancy of a zit, right?"

"Not if you're careful."

Buffy studied his face as a strange mixture of emotions rushed through her.

"How can you keep doing this?"

"It's what I was raised to do." Merrick sounded suddenly tired. "There aren't many of us left, the Watchers."

"Watchers?"

"There's a small village in Hampshire, near Stonehenge . . ."

It was obvious from Buffy's expression that she didn't have the slightest idea what he was talking about. Merrick took a deep breath and tried a simpler explanation.

". . . near a bunch of big rocks. That's where I was born. My father taught me about the training, about finding the Slayers, reading the signs. There's a small cluster of us, a few families, really. . . . Most of the neighboring villagers think we're just a bunch of harmless old loonies. I thought so myself for a long time, when I was younger. . . ."

He stopped himself and looked away.

"I'm sorry. I'm not supposed to—I shouldn't go on like this."

"I wish you would," Buffy said quietly.

"It isn't important."

"I'm curious, is all."

"Buffy, don't . . . don't start thinking of me as your friend. It interferes with the work, and it . . ."

"And it makes it worse when I die, right?"

Again the silence stretched out, heavy with hidden feelings and unspoken fears.

"Well, you know, I'm not gonna kick so easy," Buffy said at last, forcing confidence into her voice. "I've got a few things the other girls didn't have."

"What, for example?"

"Well . . . there's my keen fashion sense, for one."

Merrick rolled his eyes. "Vampires of the world, beware."

"Merrick. You made a joke." Buffy nodded, impressed. "Are you okay, I mean, do you want to lie down? I know it hurts the first time."

And in spite of himself, Merrick smiled.

19

"So they found Cassandra's body out by the railway tunnels," Jennifer said.

The whole school was buzzing with the news of Cassandra's death, and now, as Buffy and her friends made their way along the hall to class, Jennifer gave the other girls a meaningful glance.

"Nobody's saying anything, but they think she was involved in something, like, illegal or something. Like dealing."

"Well, I hope so," Kimberly retorted.

"Probably was." Jennifer looked thoughtful. "What do you suppose she was doing out there?"

"Dying," Buffy said shortly.

Jennifer wrinkled her nose. "Eeyuu."

They moved aside as several members of the basketball team came toward them, headed for the gym. Immediately the girls noticed that Jeffrey and Andy were suited up with the others, but the two boys were deep in conversation.

"And they're having some memorial service or something tomorrow," Andy told Jeffrey. "You going?"

"I don't know. Coach said I had to work on my ab's."

The boys walked on past Buffy. Without warning, Andy stopped and grabbed her from behind.

"Hey, beautiful!" Andy exclaimed, grinning.

He didn't even realize what was happening.

In a fraction of a second, Buffy flipped him over and pinned him hard against one of the lockers.

"Whoa! Whoa!" Andy conceded, struggling to free himself from Buffy's grasp. "I'm sorry. I'm *sorry*. I don't actually think you're *that* pretty."

"What's with you?" Jeffrey demanded. He and the girls were staring at Buffy like they'd never seen her before, but Buffy's attention was totally focused on Andy.

"Don't grab me, okay?" Buffy backed off, watching as Andy hurried out of her reach.

"Absolutely," Andy promised. "I see now the error of my mistake."

"Yeah, keep your hands off my woman. I'll pop you one." Jeffrey turned to Buffy with a cavalier smile. "Did he scare you?"

He slipped his arm around her, but Buffy shook it off.

"I can take care of myself, Jeffrey."

"So I noticed."

As Buffy moved off down the hall by herself, Jeffrey gazed after her with a tight smile.

"Nice to feel needed."

Andy nodded and turned back to the other players. "Let's move out!" he shouted.

"Yes!"

Jeffrey joined in the rally, but his pride was stung. Had Buffy turned around, she would have seen the hurt and humiliation on Jeffrey's face, but she kept walking and didn't look back. She didn't see Nicole and Kimberly watching her with unmistakable disdain. And she didn't see Jennifer gazing sympathetically after Jeffrey, a deep and hopeless longing in her eyes.

Buffy had more important things on her mind. Life-and-death things she could never expect these friends of hers to understand. Only Merrick understood. And as she felt herself drifting farther and farther from the people she had always depended upon, she tried to make some kind of sense out of it, if only to feel less alone.

"I mean, most of the time Jeffrey's really sweet, but sometimes he gets kind of . . . 'me Tarzan'–ish, you know what I mean?" Buffy sighed.

She had met Merrick at a trendy clothing store this afternoon. Not because Merrick wanted to, but because Buffy had insisted. Now as Merrick changed within one of the dressing stalls, Buffy stood outside the door, inspecting her fingernails as she talked to him.

"Lately it bugs me, I guess," she added lamely.

Merrick didn't answer.

"Merrick? Are you still breathing?"

From inside the cubicle, Merrick muttered, "I can't work this."

"We call them zippers." Buffy smiled to herself. "They're not supposed to be a challenge."

"But it's in the back. Why are we wasting time with this, anyway?"

"Because you clash, Merrick. You clash with everything. I mean, you might as well go around with a sign, 'Slayers trained here.' Honestly, you look like something out of . . . Pasadena."

"My clothes have always been perfectly serviceable."

"Well, you're on my turf now. You're just gonna have to trust me."

Merrick came out of the booth in multicolored parachute pants and an equally loud T-shirt. Buffy looked at him. He looked down at himself.

"I want to die," Merrick said.

"Okay," Buffy said, for once in total agreement. "The important thing is not to panic."

20

$\mathbf{P}$ike was in a hurry.

As the afternoon drew steadily on toward
twilight, he and his boss, Zeph, stood outside
Zeph's Auto Repair, while Pike worked frantically on his beat-up Dodge. He stuck his head
beneath the hood to fiddle with something,
and Zeph noticed that Pike's car was loaded
up with the boy's personal belongings.

"You said you'd have the part by two! Man,
it's almost dark."

Pike slammed the hood down. He picked up
a battered guitar case and stuffed it into his
car, then shut the door. Zeph thought for a

moment, then wiped his greasy hands on one leg of his pants.

"What nasty bug crawled up your bungus, and where are you going?" Zeph asked good-naturedly.

"I'm leaving, man." Pike's face was serious. "I'm bailing town. This place has gotten way too hairy."

"Where am I gonna find another mechanic stupid enough to work for my money?"

"Hey," Pike said, glancing at him, "have you seen Benny lately?"

"No. You want me to give him a message?"

Pike shook his head. He stared at Zeph for a long moment, then added quietly, "You should think about leaving, too, man. Sell this place . . . Something's going on here. I don't know what. Something real weird."

Pike got into his car.

The engine sputtered, then finally started up.

"Hey." Zeph looked at him curiously. "What should I do if I see Benny?"

"Run."

Pike peeled out.

In his rearview mirror, he could still see Zeph standing there watching him, and the sun burning deeper and deeper below the horizon . . .

He didn't even make it to the highway.

As night fell, the car stalled at an intersection on the very edge of town, and Pike hunched down over the wheel, listening to the rasping engine.

"Come on, come on. Don't leave me, baby. Come on, breathe."

It took him several minutes to hear the feet scraping along the pavement outside . . . several minutes to realize that someone—or something—was approaching his car.

By the time Pike finally became aware of what was happening, the creature with the hideous grin was already there on the street in front of him.

Pike had never seen Amilyn before . . .

Yet he knew with cold certainty what Amilyn was.

Pike straightened up slowly. In his rearview mirror, he could see two more figures behind him, both of them high-school age, he guessed, and with that same freshly dead look that Benny had worn. They came closer . . . taking their time. Pike waited for a second, his hand on the key.

"This is for the money, baby. Make me proud."

He turned the key again, and the car roared to life. His taillights trapped the hungry scowls of the vampires as he popped the car into reverse, smashing into the two creatures behind him. Both of them went flying, hurt but not killed.

Again Pike changed directions, flooring the accelerator, now racing at the vampire in front. As he was about to run it down, it leaped high into the air, and Pike heard a thud as something landed on top of his car. He continued to bullet down the street, trying to throw the creature off. Without warning, a hand punched through the roof and grabbed at him. Pike fought it off and desperately struggled to keep hold of the steering wheel.

The car lurched off the road, careening helplessly out of control, straight into a park.

On top of the car, Amilyn rode laughing.

Pike spotted a tree with a low branch. Still fighting to dodge Amilyn's grasp, he aimed the car as best he could at the drooping limb, and steeled himself as it got closer.

Amilyn looked up.

As the car barreled underneath the branch, there was a sudden tearing thud.

Pike saw the arm clawing down at him through the roof. For a split second it stiffened and froze, the fingers splayed wide in agony, and then it fell into his lap.

The car hit another tree dead-on. As Pike

slammed into the steering wheel, his guitar case flew through the windshield and landed on the grass beyond.

Thoroughly shaken, Pike sat still for a few moments, then slowly pulled himself from the car. He could see that he was bleeding, but it didn't seem to be as bad as he'd feared. A low, seething wail rose into the air behind him, and he turned to see Amilyn getting unsteadily to his feet.

"Oh, give me a break," Pike mumbled.

Amilyn looked down at what was left of his arm. A mangled mass of flesh hung dripping there beneath the tattered sleeve of his jacket, and he threw back his head and roared.

"I don't believe it! That was genuine leather. . . ."

He hissed furiously at Pike. Whirling around, he raced away, still snarling and wildly clutching his arm.

But the other two vampires had caught up now. As one of them moved dangerously close, Pike tried to run and felt his knees buckle beneath him, toppling him onto the ground beside his guitar case. The vampire kept coming, closing in mercilessly. Pike pulled the guitar out of the case and swung it into the vampire's head. Nothing happened. He swung and hit the creature again. The vampire batted the guitar away and grabbed Pike, lowering its face to his as the boy squirmed.

From out of nowhere, a kick blasted the vampire's head, flinging the creature to one side, where it fell. Instinctively it started up at its challenger, then gasped as Buffy slammed a stake through its heart.

Pike stared at Buffy, stunned. She pulled a walkie-talkie from her pocket and began to speak into it.

"I'm on the east side, near the playground . . . All right."

She put the instrument back into her pocket and looked down at Pike.

"Hi."

"Hi there," Pike said.

"Isn't that your car?"

"It was. I think it's pretty much ready for the—"

Pike went sprawling as the last vampire hit him from behind. Without a second's hesitation, Buffy picked up the guitar and snapped off the neck. The vampire scarcely moved before she buried the guitar neck deep in its chest and watched it fall to the ground.

Dazed, Pike saw someone run up to Buffy. It was an older man dressed in black jeans and a windbreaker, and there was something oddly familiar about him that Pike couldn't quite place. The newcomer took a long, slow look around at the decaying bodies, his gaze lingering on the one with the guitar sticking out of its chest.

"Interesting," the old guy commented, and nodded.

"I kind of had to improvise," Buffy said, and then, as she tried to help Pike to his feet, "Sorry about your guitar."

Pike was still looking at the old man. "Hey, you're the weird guy!"

"So I've been told," Merrick replied dryly.

"I know everybody here." Pike sounded pleased. "Oh. And now it's all dark . . ."

Pike's eyes glazed over as he collapsed into Buffy's arms. She held him and looked at Merrick.

"You know him?" she asked.

"Somewhat. He's very fond of passing out."

21

In the deep, secret place of Hemery High, Amilyn was in a wild frenzy.

Thrashing around the boiler room, he screamed and snarled hysterically, finally coming up to the boiler tank where he beat his one fist against the side. As the sound boomed hollowly on and on within the shadows, Lothos grabbed him and and threw him up against the wall.

"What's wrong with you?"

"My arm! He took my arm!"

"Shut up! You let him have it!"

Roughly, Lothos released him. Amilyn continued to fume, but quietly, so Lothos couldn't hear.

"You reckless imbecile," Lothos muttered. "This place is ours for the taking, and you let yourself . . . Twelve hundred years old, and you act like a child."

"I had him in my grasp!"

"Cheer up. You may still."

Only Lothos smiled at the joke. Amilyn raised the stump of his shredded sleeve and regarded it forlornly.

"I look horrible."

But Lothos was interested in more important things. "The other two—the new ones. Where are they?"

"I don't know." Amilyn sulked. "But the boy, he couldn't have killed them."

Lothos considered for a long moment. "No . . . not a boy. . . ."

Again he lost himself in deep, troubling thoughts. Several more moments went by, and finally he seemed to come to some decision. He gathered himself calmly, his voice low.

"Find out if they're dead. And do something about that arm. Honestly, I don't know how you made it through the Crusades."

He turned around and headed back through the shadows.

"Let me know about our little recruits," he

said to Amilyn as he passed through the doorway. "I'll be in my chamber. . . ."

His voice trailed away as he paused beside an oil drum and looked into the box on top.

He reached inside and plucked out a kitten.

". . . having a snack," he finished.

22

How are you doing?" Buffy asked.

She watched Pike come unsteadily through the door and into the house after her. Luckily her parents weren't around tonight to see this—she'd never have been able to explain it.

"Oh, I'm good," Pike assured her. "I'm good. Kind of miss my knees, though."

Buffy smiled at that. "You want some water or something?"

"Water. Okay."

She led the way into the kitchen, and busied herself finding a clean glass.

"Do you do this kind of thing a lot?" Pike asked. "I mean, is this, like, a hobby?"

"Not exactly."

"They were vampires, weren't they?"

Buffy nodded. "Yeah."

"Unbelievable. Vampires."

Buffy handed Pike his water, and they went back into the living room. Pike curled up in an armchair by the window. Buffy began stripping off her bloody clothes, leaving on her tank top and jeans.

"You had a car full of stuff," she remembered. "Were you leaving town?"

"Yeah, I was bailing. I have a friend, and he's really . . . well, he's really a vampire, I guess." Pike shrugged. "Bad scene."

"Well, stay here tonight."

"Thanks. Tomorrow morning, I'm on a bus. I'm gone."

"Where are you gonna go?"

"Well, I've always wanted to see Oxnard."

As Buffy glanced down at her tank top, she saw a huge, ugly gash on her arm. The bleeding had mostly stopped by now, but as she patted it carefully with her shirt, Pike suddenly noticed her injury and jumped up.

"Hey, jeez, are you okay? You need a hand?"

"It's nothing." Buffy tried to sound unconcerned. "It doesn't hurt."

Pike watched her quietly as she wrapped her shirt around her arm. When he finally spoke again, his voice bordered on awe.

"Who are you?"

Buffy didn't look up. As Pike stared at her, he saw a whole range of emotions struggle across her face, even as she fought back tears.

"I'm sorry," he said quickly, afraid he'd upset her. "I just mean . . . well, you seemed like such a flake before. But in a good way! I can just keep talking till you strike me dead, or . . ."

Buffy smiled at that, though her lips still trembled. She sat down and looked back at him helplessly, trying to get herself under control.

"Things are kind of confusing."

"I'll back that up," Pike agreed readily.

"Three weeks ago, all I thought about was . . . well, I didn't actually think about anything," Buffy began. "I definitely didn't expect this. You know what it's like when everything is suddenly . . . different? Everything you thought was crucial seems totally stupid and—"

She caught herself and broke off, gazing back at him as she suddenly realized how intently he was watching her.

"—you find yourself babbling incoherently

to a strange man in your living room," she finished, looking away.

"Are you calling me a man?"

Buffy stood up and headed toward the staircase.

"I'm kinda beat. You can stay in my mom's room if you want."

"I think I'll just hang out here." Pike settled back into his chair. "Make sure the sun comes up and everything."

"Mmkay."

She started up the stairs, but his voice stopped her.

"Hey, Buffy . . ."

"Yeah?"

"I know what it's like."

Pike watched her go up to her room. And then he stared out the window, deep in thought, deep into the night.

The bus pulled out the next morning.

As Pike stared out the window, his thoughts were as endless and heavy as the night before. He watched the terminal disappear.

Streets swept by beyond the glass. On one of them, a police officer was talking, trying to calm a hysterical man.

Next to them, on the pavement, a body lay covered by a sheet.

23

There isn't time," Merrick said.

Another of their sessions had ended, and as Buffy packed up and prepared to leave the warehouse, she continued to argue with him.

"Make time, okay? You're the one who told me to act normal." She ran a critical eye over him and thought vaguely how subdued he still looked in spite of his casual new clothes. "I've missed three practices already. If I'm not there for the Barber game tomorrow, everyone's gonna talk."

"Another distraction," Merrick said disapprovingly. "It's not right."

"Why, because it's not my fate? It's not in the Book-of-All-Knowledgefulness that I'm gonna be cheerleading at the Barber game?"

"Sooner or later you're going to have to accept it. Your fate."

"I'm pretty much learning not to accept anything anymore," Buffy grumbled. "Come on, Merrick. Basketball. Afterward we can kill and kill until there is nothing left."

She turned to go.

"None of the other girls ever gave me this much trouble," Merrick lamented.

"And where are they now?"

Buffy smiled at him and left.

The gym was packed tonight.

Buffy led the other cheerleaders perfectly through their routines, laughing and shouting, feeling almost like her old self again as the crowds rallied excitedly around her.

High up in the stands, Merrick took a seat. He had chosen another new outfit for the occasion—a letterman jacket and baseball cap —and with his binoculars hanging around his neck, he looked anything but inconspicuous amidst all the screaming teens.

On the sidelines below, Coach showed the huddled players some plays. After a brief discussion, they all clapped and broke.

"So let's *GO!*" Coach roared.

"YEAHH!"

Yelling, the team ran out onto the court while Coach turned angrily to one player who was lagging behind.

"There you are! You missed practice again. You're benched till the fourth quarter."

Coach didn't notice the look on Grueller's face as the boy walked obediently to the end of the bench and took a seat. Grinning, Grueller turned to the player next to him and spoke in a strange, passionless voice, as if repeating words phonetically.

"Go team. Rah. Go team go."

The other player, oblivious to Grueller's condition, gave him the thumbs-up and turned back to the game.

The competition was fierce. The score swung back and forth, unnervingly close. Both teams played hard and ruthlessly through the first three quarters, keeping the crowd on the very edge of their seats. By the fourth quarter, the Hemery fans were anxiously watching the scoreboard at the end of the gym.

HEMERY: 67, BARBER: 72.

A minute forty left to play.

Buffy and the cheerleaders roused the onlookers with one of their favorites:

"Two! Four! Six! Eight!
Who do we humiliate!
Barber! Barber! Yay!"

On the sidelines, Coach signaled for a player to come out, then turned to Grueller.

"Okay, you're in. Make us proud."

Grueller ripped off his sweatshirt, pulling it to shreds in his excitement. As he ran past Buffy, she winced from an unexpected pain, and her hesitation threw off the cheerleading routine, causing Nicole to practically fall over her.

"Buffy! You know these steps."

"Sorry." Buffy started cheering again, but she'd suddenly grown uneasy.

Barber had the ball on the sidelines as the whistle blew and play resumed. They threw the ball in. Grueller was there in a flash, managing a quick steal, then racing down the court, grinning madly.

Near the sideline, Jeffrey started waving his arms.

"I'm open. Grueller! I'm open!"

Grueller ignored Jeffrey and everyone else as he headed straight for the basket, knocking several guys out of his way. He jumped impressively and slammed the ball home.

The crowd went wild.

Barber took the ball out again. It got thrown in and passed up the court a couple times, then somehow Grueller was leaping through the air and intercepting the pass. Once more he made the fast break, back to his team's basket.

"Hey, open! Still open!" Jeffrey shouted. "Check it out!"

But Grueller just barreled up the court.

Buffy, watching closely, began to feel seriously concerned.

In another section of the screaming stands, Kimberly sat complaining to no one in particular.

"What is he doing? The clock's running out!" Unable to stand it anymore, she yelled, "Throw the ball!" then sat back and turned to the kid sitting beside her. "Is he so braindead?"

The boy smiled at her with a vacant stare. He waved his pennant mechanically.

And when he spoke, it was in the exact same monotone that Grueller had used.

"Rah."

Down on the court, Grueller slammed the ball home again, and the crowd roared.

HEMERY: 71, BARBER: 72.

Twenty-three seconds left.

Barber took the ball out. Someone threw it to the kid Grueller was guarding. The boy looked for a way around Grueller's huge bulk, trying to plan his move.

Grueller snarled viciously, showing a mouth full of bloody teeth.

Without hesitation, the terrified boy politely handed the ball to Grueller, then stepped back, looking sheepishly at his teammates.

Up above, Merrick peered through his binoculars at the court, and then at Buffy.

Buffy looked back at Merrick. Then she turned and focused once more on the game.

Grueller was making his way up the court, slowly this time, with almost every man on the other team guarding him. Buffy could see them all keeping their distance, as more of them began to realize just how terrifying Grueller was. She could actually hear him growling as he snapped at the other players.

Jeffrey and Andy stood at the edge of the play, doing little more than watching by now.

"Grueller's pretty much abandoned the concept of zones," Andy said offhandedly.

"Put it in, put it in . . ." Jeffrey whispered.

Grueller reached the basket with eight seconds to go. Just as he was about to shoot, an opposing player blithely stole the ball from him and made a break down the court. For a moment, Grueller looked both appalled and offended, and then, snarling ferociously, he took off after the kid with blood gleaming in his eyes.

Grueller had nearly overtaken the kid when Buffy suddenly slammed into him, sending Grueller flying.

"Girl!" a player yelled, pointing. "Girl on the court!"

From her place in the stands, Kimberly also saw Buffy and leaned forward in disbelief. "What is she *doing?*"

The strange kid beside her just stared. "Party hearty."

The clock ran out.

As the buzzer sounded, the Barber fans went absolutely wild, while around them the Hemery High kids just looked at each other, totally bemused.

Buffy and Grueller lay on the floor of the basketball court.

Ten feet apart, they stared hard into each other's eyes.

It was then that Grueller smiled—a smug, unearthly smile . . .

And Buffy knew that he knew.

Without warning, Grueller took off, running out the door.

Buffy jumped up and followed.

24

By the time Buffy got outside the gym, Grueller was already several yards away and running like the wind. She took off after him just as Merrick reached the doorway and shouted after her.

"Wait!"

But Buffy couldn't stop.

Not now.

"He knows who I am!" she yelled back, and kept going.

Grueller's speed was incredible. Buffy followed him doggedly through the dark streets, but it didn't take her long to realize she couldn't keep up. Looking around wildly for help, she spotted a biker on his Harley. She hurried up to the side of the road and tentatively stuck out her thumb. Smiling, the biker pulled to a stop in front of her.

Buffy looked down at the revving engine, at the smoke puffing thickly from twin pipes.

"Hey, babe," the biker said smoothly. "This is your lucky night."

Buffy looked at him for a long moment.

The biker landed on the ground with a thud. Buffy revved up the engine of the Harley, squealed the tires, and took off at top speed.

"What's the matter with you!" the biker screamed at her. "Too much for you to handle? Your loss, baby!"

Buffy hung on, trying to navigate the motorcycle and pick up Grueller's trail at the same time. As she roared up to a construction site, she finally spotted Grueller moving effortlessly ahead of her, and she swung sharply off the road, keeping her eyes on him, determined not to lose him again. She steered the bike on a crazy course through the site, bouncing over the rough terrain, then suddenly felt a jolt as she ran into a pile of bricks. The impact threw her headlong from the bike.

Buffy hit the ground hard.

She rolled into her fall, then struggled to get up, but couldn't.

Grueller's smiling face appeared above her.

"Fall down go boom, have to see the nurse."

"Grueller," Buffy murmured, "what did they do to you?"

Grueller lowered his face toward hers. His voice was no longer passionless. Now it boiled with evil.

"They killed me."

Without warning, he grabbed Buffy and hauled her up.

"No kidding," Buffy answered.

She head-butted him with enormous force, sending him staggering back. Before he could recover, she dived for a pile of discarded lumber and grabbed a nasty shard of wood.

As Buffy turned on Grueller, she saw two more vampires approaching her . . . stealthily surrounding her. One of them she recognized as the fan who had been sitting next to Kimberly at the game that night. He was still waving his pennant.

"The Master walks tonight," Grueller growled. "This is his kingdom now."

The vampires rushed at her. Buffy took on the first creature just as the second attacked and knocked her over. Before she could move, all three of them swarmed over her, meeting her kicks with raking claws. Helplessly, she felt herself being lifted up, held there in front of Grueller by the two other vampires, who forced her to look at him.

"You know, Buffy," Grueller snarled, smiling, "I've always wished you were mine."

Slowly he leaned toward her neck.

As the stake burst through Grueller's chest, a look of shock and surprise stiffened his face. He fell backward, dead, and Buffy stared in amazement at the figure standing there behind his body.

Pike.

Buffy felt the vampires loosen their hold. As one of them started after Pike, the boy turned and ran. Without a second's hesitation, Buffy grabbed the other vampire and flipped it over onto Grueller, impaling the creature on the same bloody stake.

Pike was yelling and running in circles, the vampire right on his heels.

"I didn't mean it!" Pike cried. "I didn't mean it!"

With the wooden shard in hand, Buffy sprinted toward them, then jumped into a series of flips. She landed with her legs around the vampire's shoulders, planting the stake into its heart as both of them toppled over onto Pike.

For a moment Pike and Buffy lay entangled with each other. They were both breathing hard, and as each of them became acutely aware of the other one's nearness, they separated and got up awkwardly, embarrassed.

"I didn't expect to see you," Buffy said.

"I know."

Buffy stared at him, unsure what to say. She wasn't facing the street, and so she didn't see Kimberly, who happened to drive by at that precise moment. As the other girl glanced out her window and noticed Buffy there with Pike, she raised an eyebrow and drove on.

"Why'd you come back?" Buffy asked finally.

"I don't know. I kind of thought I ought to be here." Pike gazed back at her. "You know, this isn't exactly the kind of thing you can run away from."

Buffy nodded. "Thanks," she said, her voice soft.

"Besides, Oxnard stinks."

They started back toward the fallen motorcycle. Pike bent over slowly to examine it.

"Listen, I . . . really do want to help. I mean, these guys are dag nasty, and my best friend is out there somewhere, and I'd like to . . . I don't know, even the score. Do some damage. I'm good with damage."

Buffy winced. As she hunched over a little, she gave a startled gasp.

"Buffy?" Pike said worriedly.

25

The biker was still there where Buffy had left him.

He was standing beside the road, trying to thumb a ride, when Merrick ran up to him.

"Did you see a girl come by here?" Merrick asked breathlessly.

"Yeah, I saw her. She took my wheels."

"Where did she go?"

"Down there. She's a psycho, man. Don't waste your time."

He pointed, and Merrick took several steps in the direction of his finger.

"Idiot girl. How long ago did—"

Merrick turned back, and his question froze on his lips.

It wasn't the biker who stood there now, not five feet away from him.

It was a tall figure . . . with a bone-white face.

"Lothos," Merrick mumbled.

The biker was on his knees. Lothos's hand was locked firmly around the kid's throat, so that the boy couldn't move or even breathe.

Merrick and Lothos regarded each other calmly.

"It's a beautiful night," Lothos spoke first. "I have never understood the human tendency to equate darkness with emptiness. To me, the black is so thick with life, like soil . . . like blood. Darkness writhes under my eyes."

He gazed thoughtfully into the shadows before speaking again.

"I remember you. She's out here as well, isn't she? Another Slayer. Who is it this time? What offering have you brought me?"

Lothos let go of the biker. The boy fell over on the ground, limp and lifeless.

"It doesn't really matter," Lothos went on. "The names, the faces, they all melt together. After a time, there really is no difference. One more pathetic girl, just begging for me to end it."

"This one may surprise you," Merrick said.

"I rather doubt it, if she was raised here."

"She's not like the others. Doesn't play our way. It's a rare quality; I don't think she even knows how strong she is."

"Such drooling sentiment from a Watcher. I'm all aglow," Lothos mocked him. "Surely she's not that special. The girl in Budapest, now she had spirit. Do you remember when I owed you her heart?"

Before Merrick could respond, Buffy came running out of the trees nearby, stopping dead in her tracks some thirty feet away from the two men. Startled, Merrick and Lothos turned their heads toward the intrusion.

"Get away from here, girl," Merrick ordered quickly, pretending not to know her. "This man is dangerous."

Buffy's eyes went wide as they locked on Lothos. He held her in a long stare, and then he smiled back at Merrick.

There was deep, cold knowing in his eyes.

"What have we here?" Lothos purred.

"I mean it," Merrick said again, more sternly this time. He was watching Buffy, but the girl seemed frozen, unable to move. "Get out!"

Buffy's lips barely opened. "I . . ."

Lothos took a step toward her, his eyes

sweeping her up and down in a leisurely inspection.

"All this . . . for me?"

"Leave her," Merrick demanded. "If you want a soul, take mine."

Lothos gave him a disdainful look. "I don't make deals. I want the girl."

He turned his attention back to Buffy as Pike roared up beside her on the bike. Still paralyzed, Buffy didn't even seem to realize Pike was there. She kept her gaze full on Lothos as the vampire continued his slow, steady approach.

"You're not ready for this!" Merrick broke in, trying to jar Buffy, to get her attention. "Go!"

"I think she's ready." Lothos sounded smug.

He held out his hand to Buffy as the distance narrowed between them. From the expression on Buffy's face, Merrick couldn't tell if she was entranced or terrified or both.

Pike reached over and shook her, hard.

"Come on!"

"Girl," Merrick begged, "for once in your life . . ." His voice trailed away as he saw a glimmer of recognition on Buffy's face. And as she focused on him at last, he finished hopefully, ". . . do as you're told."

He almost smiled at her.

A wise smile full of sorrow.

Buffy snapped back to reality and stepped toward the bike behind her.

Merrick and Pike looked straight into each other's eyes. In that one powerful moment, it was as though some secret understanding passed between them. . . .

Then Merrick's lips moved in a silent command.

"Go."

Lothos was ready for them.

As Buffy jumped on the bike, Lothos came swiftly behind her, gliding like wind through the dark. Pike revved the engine, but Lothos was on them in an instant. So intent was he on Buffy that he paid no attention to Merrick in back of him as the old man gracefully whipped out a gun.

Merrick fired into Lothos's back—again—and again.

Lothos stumbled—and Pike and Buffy peeled out from beneath his grasp. Unhurt but furious, he turned on Merrick, his eyes falling on the gun in Merrick's hand.

"You insult me with that!"

"Distract you," Merrick corrected him. "You'll not have this one, not this time."

Lothos regained his composure. He started toward Merrick, even though the old man still held the gun at arm's length, pointed at him.

"I have her face," Lothos said. "And after I make you mine, you will give me her name."

"Not in this life."

"Exactly. Everything will come to me in time."

Merrick's voice dropped to a near-whisper, tight with intensity. "Get thee behind me!"

"I told you," Lothos said, smiling, "I'm not the Evil One."

"Then I'll deal with him."

Merrick pulled the gun back and pointed it at himself.

The last thing he saw was the startled look on Lothos's face as the shot rang out.

Far away, on the back of the speeding bike, Buffy shut her eyes, burying her head in Pike's back as the gunshot faded into the night.

Had they not been moving so fast, she might have heard something else several moments later. . . .

As Merrick's body fell heavily to the ground in front of Lothos, the vampire looked down, his face twisted in disgust and disappointment.

And then he let out a hissing roar . . . louder . . . louder . . . his unearthly cry trembling the night around him with its promise of revenge.

26

Morning sunlight poured in through the dirty windows of the warehouse as Buffy wandered about aimlessly. She was still wearing her cheerleader uniform, and she hadn't slept all night.

She could see Merrick's personal belongings piled on an old crate in a corner. She walked over and stood there, rummaging slowly through them. Maps ... newspaper clippings ... a battered passport with stamps from a dozen countries and a classically unflattering picture of Merrick, his eyes and mouth half open. A stupid souvenir he had obviously picked up at the airport—a glass ball enclosing the L.A. skyline that snowed when you shook it. Buffy stared at the glass ball for a long time before picking up one last thing.

It was a small wooden cross, rough, but intricately carved.

She put it back on top of Merrick's other stuff.

Awkwardly, Buffy knelt, shutting her eyes and thinking hard for several seconds.

She started to pray. "I'm supposed to say something, but you're just way dead, you know. You're deeply dead. And . . ."

She sat down heavily on the floor.

"And I don't know what to do. You were the one who . . . I don't know if the training was over. I don't even know if I passed. You're so stupid! How could you be so stupid! What am I supposed to do without you!"

She stopped and looked down for a moment.

"Amen."

27

In the Hemery High gym, a banner was stretched across the central beam of the ceiling. Huge letters proclaimed: "THE EARTH IS OUR HOME," while a half dozen inflatable globes dangled nearby. Nicole and Kimberly were busy setting up the drinks table, unloading and stacking hundreds of Styrofoam cups. Jennifer walked by, balancing a load of plastic wrappings and containers in her arms.

"I got all the plastic stuff," Jennifer greeted them. "What should I do with it?"

Kimberly stared at her like she was a total idiot. "Throw it out."

She watched as Jennifer went on past, then resumed her conversation with Nicole.

"It really was mondo bizarro," Nicole said.

"Oh, please!" Kimberly looked exasperated. "When she ran onto the court in the middle of the game? Was that the most out-of-it thing ever, or did I blink?"

"Way mental," Nicole agreed.

As the two girls started to giggle, Kimberly was the first to notice Buffy walking into the gym. Kimberly and Nicole took one look at Buffy's ragged clothes and weary expression, and immediately stopped laughing.

"Hi, Buffy," Kimberly spoke up.

"Hi, guys."

"You were supposed to be here at three," Kimberly reminded her.

"I forgot."

"Buffy, what is your sitch?" Kimberly complained. "You're acting like the Thing from Another Tax Bracket; it's too weird."

"Look, a lot's been going on," Buffy tried to explain. "That's what I wanted to tell you guys about. I need to tell you. You see . . . a while ago, I met this guy—"

"You have another boyfriend," Kimberly said seriously.

"Cool!" Nicole looked pleased.

"Does Jeffrey know?" Jennifer asked, coming up beside them.

"It's not that at all." Buffy shook her head. "This is an old guy, he's like fifty."

Kimberly and Nicole exchanged looks. "Eeyuu."

"No, no. Listen," Buffy insisted. "Haven't you guys noticed how weird things have gotten around here? Like, people disappearing, people turning up dead . . ."

"What are you talking about?" Nicole sounded totally bewildered, while Kimberly shrugged in agreement.

"Weird? You mean like you hanging out with that Poke guy? I saw you last night after the game."

"Pike," Buffy said.

"You're having a fling with him?" Nicole looked shocked.

"He doesn't look fifty," Jennifer mused.

"Guys. Guys!" Buffy's voice rose. "Reality pulled out of here five minutes ago."

"Oh, thank you very much," Kimberly retorted.

"Like you've got a grip." Nicole frowned.

"You're so out of it," Jennifer joined in. "You've blown off cheerleading, you've blown off the dance committee . . ."

Buffy looked at them as though she couldn't believe what she was hearing. "Excuse me for having something important to do."

"This isn't important?" Kimberly challenged her angrily. "This is the dance."

"Right." Buffy held her ground. "It's a *dance*. It's a stupid dance with a bunch of stupid kids that I see every stupid day."

"So, we're stupid now?" Nicole lifted her chin indignantly.

"You know, just because you're going through a life crisis doesn't mean you have to drag us into it," Kimberly added, just as upset. "This isn't just any dance. It happens to be the last dance of our last year. Look, Buffy, you want to play house with the unwashed masses, that's fine. But personally, I think you ought to spend a little time prioritizing. I really do."

"Listen to you." Buffy stared at her. "What language are you speaking?"

"Get out of my facial." Kimberly turned and stormed out.

"Well, I guess you got what you came for," Nicole added nastily.

"Nicole—"

"Later for it," Nicole cut her off abruptly.

Buffy stood there watching as Nicole and Jennifer huffed out of the gym.

She stood there for a long, long time . . . alone and very small amid the bright party streamers.

28

Buffy propped herself against the kitchen sink, vacantly rinsing a glass. She stared down at it, watching the mechanical movement of her hands, seeing nothing at all. She hardly even noticed when her mother breezed through the kitchen door.

"Dinner's in the fridge, stay away from the Jag, we'll be back by twelve."

Buffy's mother stopped. She looked at her daughter curiously.

"Buffy, honey?"

"Yeah?"

And suddenly, more than anything, Buffy wanted to talk, wanted to tell her mother the whole horrible, unbelievable truth. She looked up hopefully and saw her mother's concerned frown.

"Have you gained a few pounds?" Her mother narrowed her eyes. "Maybe it's that outfit . . ."

"Maybe." Buffy turned back to the sink.

"What's Bobby gonna say?"

"I don't know, Mom. I've never met Bobby."

Buffy's mom laughed. "Aren't we the chatty ones. Kiss noise."

She hurried out the door.

Buffy looked down at her clothes and at herself, and came to a firm decision.

The last person Buffy expected to see that night was Pike.

As she made her way through the crowded mall, his tall, lean frame suddenly appeared out of nowhere, and he hurried to catch up.

"Buffy, hey, I've been looking all over for you."

Buffy kept walking. Pike amiably kept pace beside her.

"I been working on some stuff for you. Whatcha doing?"

"I'm going shopping," Buffy said brusquely. "Don't try to stop me."

"Cool." Pike nodded. "I could actually use a couple of allen wrenches. So what do you need?"

"A dress."

"Dress, huh? What for?"

"For the dance."

"Come again?"

"I'm going to the senior dance."

Pike pretended to play charades. "Second word . . . sounds like 'dance.'"

Buffy stopped right next to a photo booth.

"I'm going to the dance."

"What for?"

"In order to dance and to drink punch and to be with my friends. *Comprende?*"

"I don't believe this." Pike looked mildly amazed. "The world's under attack by the legions of the undead, and you're going to a mixer?"

"It's not a mixer." Buffy bristled. "It's the senior dance. And it's important. You wouldn't understand."

"You got that right. I thought you wanted to kill vampires."

"I don't want to kill anybody, and I don't want to talk about it anymore."

"Listen," Pike said seriously, "it stinks, what happened to Merrick. I know that."

Buffy shrugged. "He did what he was supposed to." Her tone was offhand, almost disdainful.

"But, Buffy, you're the guy, the chosen guy."

"Right," Buffy retorted. "I'm the chosen one. And I *choose* to be shoppping."

"I should have known."

Buffy raised her fist, and Pike started back involuntarily.

"Leave me alone," Buffy said.

"Benny was right." Pike stared at her. "You guys are all exactly the same."

Buffy turned on her heel and walked away, but she could still hear Pike calling after her.

"I'm not disappointed, I'm just angry."

As Buffy disappeared among the shoppers, Pike headed off in the other direction.

He didn't look back at the photo booth. . . .

If he had, he would have seen Benny emerging from the curtains, gazing after them with incredulous glee.

"Buffy?" Benny repeated to himself. *"Buffy?"*

He moved off quickly into the crowd.

One second after he left, a strip of photos dropped into the slot.

There was no one in them.

29

In the boiler room beneath Hemery High, the vampires had gathered. Lothos stood with Benny, who was positively beaming at his latest accomplishment.

"Astonishing, for one so fresh," Lothos said admiringly. "And you know where she lives?"

Benny shook his head. "No, Master. But I know what she's doing Saturday night."

Lothos let his eyes sweep slowly across the shadows, over all the hideous faces waiting there.

He smiled and put his arm around Benny.

"It's good to be dead."

30

It took Buffy a long time to find just the right dress.

All the outfits she would normally have gone crazy over now seemed uncomfortably tight and even bizarre for her newly acquired fashion tastes. She spent most of Saturday looking. When she finally decided on the perfect one, she took it home and laid it out on her bed.

She stuffed her bloodstained clothes into a duffel bag along with some stakes. Then she tossed the bag into the back of her closet, and started getting ready for the dance.

The party was already under way when

Buffy got to the gym. Streamers fluttered everywhere, and tables had been set up along the windows. As couples danced, a deejay spun tunes and kept up a stream of senseless chatter. There was a setup in one corner for taking pictures. Kids who were all used to seeing each other every day looked conspicuously different tonight—very elegant and hip—dressed in every imaginable shade of black. Nicole and Kimberly, both wearing slinky little black dresses, were standing by the punch bowl and talking.

As Buffy entered the gym in her long white strapless gown, she suddenly felt too conservative for this crowd, almost as if she'd gone too far trying to be normal. She clutched her matching purse and walked in hesitantly, looking around for Jeffrey, but saw Andy instead.

"Buffy!" he greeted her. "Looking tasty!"

"Thanks. Have you seen Jeffrey?"

But Andy had moved on.

Buffy worked her way slowly through the crowd and over to the punch bowl. Nicole and Kimberly abruptly stopped whispering.

"Hi, guys." Buffy smiled.

"Hi."

"Have you guys seen Jeffrey? The limo never showed, I thought he might be here."

Nicole and Kimberly gave each other a significant look.

"I haven't seen him tonight," Nicole said.

"Oh." Buffy picked up a glass of punch and went on pleasantly, "I'm glad you guys are here. It's good to see you."

Kimberly's voice dripped sarcasm: "Yeah, whoops, I came."

Buffy paused, then tried again. "You look way pretty, Kim."

"I know. I like your little outfit."

"It's amazing what you can do with a parachute and some starch," Nicole added.

"As long as there's room for three in it," Kimberly kept it up. "What, didn't you bring your new friends?"

Buffy stared at them, startled by their attack. Nicole giggled.

"I guess you guys are mad at me," Buffy admitted. "I'm sorry. I've been really—"

Jeffrey suddenly appeared between them with Jennifer on his arm.

"Jeffrey!" Buffy brightened. "There you are. I—"

Her words choked in her throat. She could see everybody staring at her—at Jeffrey—at Jennifer—assessing the situation. She could feel the expression on her own face, the shock slowly fading to deep hurt. Jeffrey looked uncomfortable; Jennifer was practically apoplectic with embarrassment. Buffy could hear Kimberly giggling uncontrollably beside her, while Nicole was able to manage a bit more restraint.

"Buffy," Jeffrey finally spoke up, "what are you doing here?"

"I thought we were meeting here," Buffy said lamely.

"I'm here with Jenny."

As Buffy glanced over at her friend, Jennifer seemed to be hyperventilating, tugging at Jeffrey's arm like a dog on a leash.

"I don't understand," Buffy mumbled.

"Oh, come on, Buffy. You know what's going on," Jeffrey said defensively. "It's not working out at all. I've got to move on. I mean, I've got needs, too. I told you about all this."

"No, you didn't. When?"

"Didn't you get my message?"

"You broke up with my machine?"

"You weren't home." Jeffrey's tone was self-righteous now. "Like always."

"You left me a *message?*"

"I'm out of here. Jenny."

At the mention of her name, Jennifer jumped, and in her haste to get away she bumped Buffy's arm, spilling bright red punch down the other girl's chest. Horrified, Jennifer fled with Jeffrey in tow. As they left the gym, Kimberly found the whole predicament funnier than ever, but Nicole was silent.

Buffy turned to the wall as a soft ballad came over the speakers. Tears filled her eyes, and she wiped futilely at her dress. After a long time, she gathered herself together and looked after Jeffrey and Jennifer toward the door.

Pike was there.

He was walking in, alone, wearing a leather jacket and baggy old tuxedo pants, accented with chains, an earring, and unlaced sneakers.

He looked great.

As Pike cut through the crowds and walked directly toward Buffy, she could see a few heads turning, following his progress across the floor.

"I crashed your party." Pike looked down at her.

"Pretty shallow of you."

"That's me."

"I'm glad you came."

"Yeah, you look like you're having a swell time."

Noticing the stain on Buffy's dress, Pike picked up a glass of punch. He looked around the room, and without hesitation dumped the punch down the front of his shirt. Buffy smiled at him.

"Will I get my head knocked off if I ask you to dance?" Pike asked.

Buffy shook her head. "I don't actually think Jeffrey's gonna notice."

Pike took her into his arms and began to lead slowly, not too close.

"Yeah, well, you're the one I'm afraid of," Pike teased.

They danced for a while without speaking, their bodies moving closer and closer.

"You know," Pike finally said, "you're not like the other girls."

Buffy pulled him nearer. She held him gently, her whisper almost weak in his ear.

"Yes, I am."

All around them, couples danced and kissed.

Gary Murray stood along the wall and kept watch.

At a table beside the windows, Kimberly sat with her bovine date and watched Buffy disdainfully.

"I can't believe it," she muttered.

Without warning, the window shattered by her head.

As Kimberly screamed and jumped back, a vampire's hand clawed through the broken glass and reached for her.

31

Other windows broke and shattered. As glass sprayed around the gym, more and more vampires appeared outside, surrounding the dancers and grinning hungrily. A couple of students ran for the inner door, but it was locked tight from the other side.

A confused awareness was rippling through the crowd now, as everyone slowly became aware that something strange was happening. The noise and music faded and died, and kids began herding vaguely and fearfully into the middle of the room.

Buffy and Pike looked around, assessing the situation.

A student staggered in through the outer door, screaming and holding his neck.

"They're out there! They're vampires! Somebody help me!"

He fell to the ground, a few feet inside the doorway. For one horrible second, nobody moved. Then one of the students started toward the body.

"Don't go near the door," Buffy warned him.

Instead, Buffy ran over and checked the corpse, then lifted her head, listening as a number of heavy footsteps began to lurch through the mist toward the gym.

Buffy stepped back as three teenage vampires lumbered up to the door.

"It's party time," the first one declared, licking his lips.

"Don't worry!" Buffy called back to the crowd. "They can't come in here. They can't come in unless they're invited."

"I already invited them," Kimberly said.

Every face in the room turned to look at her. As Kimberly met their accusing stares, she drew herself up defensively.

"They're seniors!"

Pike reached into an inner pocket and pulled out a handful of small stakes he'd made.

151

He gave them to Buffy, and she opened her purse.

Inside, amid all the cosmetics, hair spray, keys, gum, water bottle and pens lay Merrick's wooden cross. Buffy shifted everything aside and fitted the stakes in, thinking out loud.

"The first thing we should—"

"Buffy," the first vampire drooled, "you wanna dance?"

"Looks like you're busted," Pike said to her.

The second vampire crowded the door, his eyes gleaming. "We want her! We want Buffy! Send her out."

"Or we come in," the first vampire promised.

They faded back, almost disappearing. Pike looked out the window, where more vampires were gathering around the gym.

"All right, everybody stay calm." Gary Murray held up his hands for quiet and focused his attention on Buffy. "What's going on?"

"Looks bad, Buffy," Pike said matter-of-factly.

One of the senior girls spoke up. "Send her out."

"What?" Buffy stared at her.

"They'll kill us!" Kimberly agreed. "She's the one they're mad at!"

"Yeah," one of the boys echoed. "Send her out!"

"Everybody, be quiet!" Gary Murray tried to keep order.

"What, are you kidding? They'll kill her!" Andy burst out, appalled.

"They'll kill *us*!" Kimberly reminded him.

Pike moved toward Kimberly with his fist raised. "You want some punch?"

"I got detention slips here." Gary Murray waved them in the air. "I'm not afraid to use them. . . ."

But other students had picked up the cry now, clamoring to sacrifice Buffy. Pike crossed over to his bag, which he'd left beside the door. As two boys moved toward Buffy, Andy quickly intervened. Pike stepped in front of her, holding his custom-made cartridge-load crossbow, and trained it on the crowd. Then he stood there calmly and waited until the room quieted down.

"There's gotta be a back way out of here, or something," Pike suggested.

Buffy gazed around the room.

She saw a happy celebration that had suddenly turned deadly . . . She saw the partygoers—her friends—staring back at her, angry and scared. She looked out the door. Then back again at her friends.

"I'm going out the front," she said.

"Are you nuts, Buffy?" Even Pike was staring at her now. "There's dozens of them out there. They'll rip us apart."

Buffy shook her head. "You're staying here." She saw the look on his face, but before he could speak, she rushed on. "Some of them might not come after me. If they don't, this place is gonna turn into a total stain."

Pike coolly regarded the crowd. "You say that like it's a bad thing."

"Buffy, this is crazy," Andy argued. "What do these guys want?"

"Andy, start breaking up some chairs. You'll need weapons." Buffy held her ground and stared back at him, relieved when he obediently moved off. She went to Pike's bag and started pulling out stakes. "Good thing one of us was prepared."

But Pike wasn't listening. "Buffy, there's no way you're going out there alone."

Buffy stood up.

Before Pike could say another word, she kissed him hard on the lips.

"Don't make me mad."

And as Pike watched speechlessly, she knelt down and began to rip the hem of her dress.

32

Outside, a mist had risen around the gym, swirling about the feet of the undead who stood clustered near the door. There looked to be about twenty of them now, some with keen, eager expressions, others vacant and half-conscious with bloodlust. They watched . . . and they waited.

Buffy appeared in the doorway. The vampires saw her walk slowly out into the open. Her torn dress came to just above her knees, and she wore Pike's leather jacket over it. Her purse was strapped across her chest under the jacket. In one hand she held Pike's crossbow; in her other hand was a cross. As she stepped farther away from the door, the vampires began to close around her.

She heard the door shut at her back.

The vampires came closer . . . still closer. They began to circle her, while she stood there and tried to anticipate their next move. She waited until they were about eight feet away, and then she whipped out a bottle of Perrier and sprayed it all around herself, searing the first line of vampires. Screaming, they clutched their faces.

In an astounding blur of gymnastics and martial arts, Buffy held her own, leaping, throwing kicks and punches, and driving an occasional stake expertly into its target. She managed to scatter the vampires just long enough to make a run for it.

From the windows of the gym, everyone watched as the vampires followed Buffy.

"It's okay!" Kimberly called out excitedly. "I think they're going after her!"

As if it had heard, one of the vampires turned back toward the gym, its mouth fixed in a huge grin. Behind it, at least half the other vampires turned and started back, eager for the easy pickings inside.

Pike stared at Kimberly. "I'll bet you feel stupid."

"Let's get away from these windows!" Gary Murray ordered. "Find something to cover them with."

Immediately the students started moving, grabbing whatever they could find.

"Bring over the table," Pike said, and Nicole glanced anxiously around the room.

"There's nails and stuff we used to put everything up," she told him.

"Get 'em."

Andy and some others dragged a table across the floor. Pike helped them hoist it up against the window. He looked out one last time through the glass, then covered it up.

Buffy was racing across the campus now, the undead close on her heels. Running as fast as she could to a nearby cluster of school buildings, she passed a line of parked cars and recognized Jeffrey's BMW on one end. She sped by it, but even as she did so, she could hear the voices through its windows.

"You and Jennifer deserve each other," she said dryly. "Oops!"

Glancing up again, she saw the vampires closer than ever, and she took off with the horde right behind her.

* * *

In the gym, disaster struck quickly.

To everyone's horror, windows began to explode, the boards over them splintering and smashing inward. At one window, a student frantically pounded in nails, but was caught and dragged out, screaming for his life.

One vampire, trying to crawl in, was immediately skewered by Pike. Another managed to make it through, but was smashed on the head repeatedly by Andy. It staggered, smiling, then turned toward the boy.

"The heart!" Pike yelled. "Stab them in the heart!"

Andy shoved a table leg into the creature's chest just as it closed its fingers around his throat.

Kimberly shrieked as a vampire grabbed her and started forcing her out a window. In a frenzy, Nicole ran to her, trying to wrestle the vampire's hands away.

The vampire grabbed Nicole instead.

Thrown off balance, she was almost out the window before Kimberly could even react. Helplessly, Kimberly began screaming for help. Andy and Pike dashed to the window, but it was too late.

As Nicole was dragged out into the night, vampires swarmed over her.

Behind the record player, another vampire was looking for music. He stopped, finding a record he liked, and put it on.

The soft strains of "Teen Angel" wafted out over the butchery in the gym. Beneath fluttering party decorations, the grisly festivities seemed dreamy and surreal.

Hearing the music, another vampire grabbed Kimberly and started to dance with her, ignoring her hysterical shrieks. As it leaned forward to bite her neck, Pike stabbed it through from the back. For a moment he watched the creature's death agonies, and then he turned and froze.

He was face to face with Benny.

33

As Buffy approached the building nearest to the gym, she could still see about twenty vampires behind her. Finding the door locked, she smashed it with her shoulder and ran inside.

Several vampires started to follow her into the building, but a figure suddenly appeared before them and raised its hand, stopping them all in their tracks. The creatures stared in silence, and slowly began to fade back.

Amilyn smiled at them.

He raised his fingers to his lips.

"Sshhhh . . ."

* * *

Benny slammed Pike down onto a table, lowering his ghastly face within inches of his friend's. In the background, "Teen Angel" had been replaced by hard rock music.

"Isn't this great, Pike?" Benny grinned. "Isn't it great? Finally got those rich girls on the run."

He hoisted Pike up and backhanded him across the jaw, sending Pike flying against a wall. Pike shook his head as Benny came at him again.

Benny wasn't smiling anymore.

"Of *course* I'm angry!" Benny raged. "I leave you alone for five minutes, and look who you're hanging out with!"

He whirled around and grabbed a girl, yelling into her face.

"I don't want girls with good taste, I want a girl that tastes good!"

The girl promptly fainted. Benny dropped her and turned back to Pike, who was getting shakily to his feet, blood trickling down his forehead.

"I was gonna change you, man." Benny glared at him. "I was gonna give you life! Do you know what that means?"

Behind them, Gary Murray was still yelling orders at students, holding a board up against a window as vampires pounded on it from outside. The exposed part of the window shattered, raining glass down on his head.

Buffy moved quickly along the dark hallway, then crouched near a window and peered out.

Nothing.

She let her eyes sweep up and down the corridor, over blank doorways, steeling herself for an attack. She checked her purse.

Her junk was still there, as well as Merrick's cross. But there were no stakes left.

Muttering under her breath, Buffy moved swiftly into a classroom.

Pike backed away as Benny approached him. Benny stalked slowly, ruthlessly, and as Pike went by an overturned table, he noticed the stubs of its broken legs sticking up toward the ceiling.

"Never die," Benny said. "Never get kicked around, never get busted."

Benny grabbed Pike with hasteful force. His fingers dug into Pike's arms, deep and sharp enough to draw blood.

"It means *never* having to say you're sorry! And you blow it all off with that stupid girl? What about *my* needs!"

Without warning, Pike grabbed Benny, holding him close in a brotherly embrace. He saw Benny's surprised look of confusion.

Still holding him, Pike pitched forward onto the table, driving the leg shard through Benny's back. Benny twitched and screamed in Pike's arms as he felt himself dying.

Pike held him for a long time.

And then he let his friend go.

He stood up, dazed and sad. He looked lost.

A window shattered far behind him, and as the sound registered at last, Pike pulled his eyes back into focus and went to help.

Sitting by a wall, tiny and silent amid the blood and carnage, sat Kimberly.

34

Buffy couldn't hear a sound.

Still moving cautiously, she headed for the window of the classroom and lowered the shade. She crouched behind the teacher's desk and pulled the chair down next to her, laying it on its side.

She slammed her elbow down on the chair leg. It was a very controlled and efficient motion, and the leg snapped right off. She looked around once more to make certain that no one had heard her, and then she picked up her new weapon.

She went cautiously to the door and peered out.

Right beside her, Amilyn's face materialized out of the shadows, his gleaming eyes following the direction of her stare.

"All clear?" Amilyn whispered.

Buffy screamed and spun around. She felt a sick jolt as Amilyn hit her and sent her flying back into the classroom. The stake sailed out of her hand, landing on a desk by the window.

Buffy did not land nearly as well. She crashed into a row of desks and wrenched her leg badly. Amilyn gave his most repulsive laugh and advanced toward her.

"Pleased to meet you! Won't you guess my"—he kicked her violently—"name?"

Buffy glared at him, defiant through her pain, "It wouldn't be Stumpy, would it?"

He kicked her again.

"How about Lefty?"

"You're a fool, bloodbag, and now you'll die a fool!"

Amilyn grabbed her by the neck with his one arm and pinned her against the wall in the corner. Buffy groped wildly for the stake, but it was just out of reach. She could feel Amilyn squeezing the life out of her, could smell the stench of his breath, his face only inches away from her own.

"The chosen one," he mocked. "You're just another bloodbag—not even fit to die for the Master. When will you ever learn?"

Buffy looked about frantically for help.

She saw the bottom of the window shade, the pull dangling aimlessly. She struggled to get her words out.

"I do know . . . one thing. . . ."

"What?" Amilyn sneered.

"I know . . . what time sunrise is."

Summoning all her strength, she yanked down on the shade pull and let it go.

"No!" Amilyn screamed.

He turned in horror, releasing Buffy, trying to catch the shade. The instant she was free, Buffy grabbed the stake and, in one swift motion, buried it in Amilyn's back.

The shade went up, flapping loudly as it spun.

Beyond the windowpane, it was still pitch black.

Wide-eyed, silent, Amilyn gazed deep into the night, feeling his life flow away.

"It's in about four hours, fool," Buffy said softly.

Amilyn spun around, dying rage in his eyes. He grabbed Buffy, his strength terrifying even as his body began to smoke. Suddenly shrieking, he hurled the two of them onto the ground with such incredible power that they went crashing through the floorboards below.

35

Helplessly, Buffy and Amilyn fell through the ceiling and plunged into the pool of blood.

Amilyn's body surfaced first, now only a husk.

Buffy struggled up next to him, waist-deep in the thick, red gore. She was soaked through with blood, and her wounds hurt more than ever. Breathing hard, she stood there for a moment . . . and then her eyes went wide.

"Oh, please, no . . . not yet. . . ."

Lothos rose gracefully from the pool.

He was smiling.

As he held her with his calm stare, Buffy gazed back at him, paralyzed with fear.

"I knew you'd come," Lothos said, and began to move toward her, the blood lapping at his sides. "You knew it, too, didn't you? All your life, dreaming . . . waiting to feed me."

At the mention of her fate, Buffy was galvanized into action. She threw several punches at Lothos, but he took them without flinching. She grabbed desperately at what remained of Amilyn and began to pull on the stake still wedged in his chest. Lightning quick, Lothos closed his hand around hers, squeezing until the stake splintered and Buffy screamed in pain. With one fluid movement, he knocked her down into the dark red slime.

Buffy struggled up and tried to back away from him, but it was almost impossible to wade through the sluggish gore. She saw Lothos look down at Amilyn's corpse, as if he were contemplating it, and then his face darkened.

"Ah, my fool is dead," Lothos said softly. "He was careless, always. Still, I'll pull out your tongue for that."

Buffy saw his eyes focus upon her once more. Again she backed up; again he came toward her.

"Don't you understand?" Lothos went on. "I've killed you a dozen times. Your life is not a blink of my eye, not a single breath. I have

lived in the shadows, in the pulsing filth behind men's eyes, a thousand years and more. I
have conversed with the worms that fed on my
corpse, and I have bathed in the blood of
emperors."

Buffy lifted her chin. "Have you ever thrown
up in the front row of a Richard Marx con-
cert?" she remarked, her voice breaking the
spell of his reverie.

"What?"

And she was up and out of the pool and
turning to run, Lothos momentarily thrown by
her insolence.

Even then, she didn't get far.

Lothos was on her the very second she
emerged into the boiler room from his chamber. He grabbed her by the hair and threw her
to the floor.

"You waste time. That is a sin."

Slowly he knelt over her as Buffy groped
frantically in her purse. She could feel his
awesome power, his disdain as he looked her
over and smiled.

"You're even weaker than the others,"
Lothos murmured.

"I think you've forgotten something."

Buffy pulled out the small cross and thrust it
in front of him. Lothos snarled, then grabbed
it, his hand trapping hers. As the cross burst

into flames, he held Buffy's hand tightly, agonizingly, in the fire.

"This?" he spat at her. "This is your only weapon! Your puny faith?"

"No . . ." With her other hand, Buffy quickly held up her hair spray. "My keen fashion sense."

She aimed the can at him and squeezed, the spray igniting from the burning cross. A jet of flame whooshed right into his face. Lothos screamed and released her, lurching backward.

His head was on fire.

Buffy scrambled up and hobbled away, determined not to look back.

With his head hideously aflame, Lothos stumbled wildly about his chamber, then pitched forward with a thick splash into the pool.

It took Buffy a few minutes to find her way out of the boiler room. When she came out at last, she limped along the corridor as quickly as she could.

"This is the stupidest dance I have *ever* been to," she muttered. "It's not even a contest."

She reached a locked door that said GYMNASIUM: AUTHORIZED PERSONNEL ONLY. She put her shoulder to it and pushed.

In Lothos's chamber, the Vampire-King pulled himself out of the sweet, heavy blood. His head was charred and torn almost beyond recognition, and when he screamed, his cry was thick with rage.

The scream filled the hallway.

As Buffy shoved at the heavy metal door, she suddenly froze, then turned wide-eyed at the unearthly sound.

"Oops."

And she could hear him now, coming out of his chamber . . . through the boiler room . . . along the hall. . . .

She could hear him, chasing after her. . . .

He was moving much too fast to be only running.

36

Inside the gym, the battle was nearly over.

Pike struggled with the last vampire, holding on tightly while another student rammed a stake into the creature's heart. As the vampire died, Pike dropped it at his feet and looked slowly around the room.

They seemed to have won at last.

There were no more vampires loose in the gym. While some kids took care of the wounded, they kept their eyes on the windows, still on the lookout for further attacks. Kimberly sat by a wall, her eyes wide and empty.

The door to the hall was boarded up, a table nailed to its surface and junk piled in front.

One boy looked out through the small window at the top, then turned and yelled.

"Hey! Come here!"

Immediately, Pike rushed over to the door. Andy, holding a rag to a wound on his neck, joined him. Together they pressed their faces to the glass and peered out into the dim light beyond.

The long corridor was lined with gray lockers. At the other end of the hallway, Buffy was coming through a door that led to the cellar. She practically collapsed back onto it to shut it behind her, and then she looked around nervously.

Pike banged on the gym door. "Buffy!" He glanced at Andy, then back at the barricade. "Help me get this open."

Kimberly stood up slowly, shaking her head. "Don't let her in! Don't let her in!"

But Pike and Andy ignored her and began to move stuff away from the door. To their surprise, several other kids rushed up to help as Pike pulled at the tabletop.

"They'll kill us!" Kimberly shouted hysterically. "Get her out!"

Gary Murray stopped in front of Kimberly. He put his hand over her face and pushed her against the wall. Cross-eyed, she slid back down into silence.

Out in the hallway, Buffy started limping toward the gym. She could see the door ahead of her, yet it seemed impossibly far away. She tried to concentrate on reaching it, but she kept glancing back over her shoulder, toward the door through which she had just escaped.

Working feverishly, Pike and Andy and the others almost had the gym door cleared now.

Buffy was more than halfway there, still watching behind her.

And then, abruptly, the cellar door began to shake.

Pike felt the rumbling and looked about in confusion. It came from beneath and all around, a deep ominous sound.

Almost to the gym now, Buffy felt it, too.

She looked back once more, and saw the cellar door trembling violently.

As Buffy tried to cross the last ten feet to the gym, she saw Pike and Andy pull the door wide open. Then, in a sudden explosion of concrete and plaster, Lothos erupted from the floor in front of her, floating there and seething with anger.

"You!"

He grabbed her and hurled her the length of the hall. As Buffy slammed into someone's locker, it burst open and spilled a notebook out onto the floor. The binder fell open, revealing a plastic case inside, loaded with pens and pencils.

Drained and hurting, Buffy propped herself up as best she could and looked about her. There was nothing wooden anywhere, nothing sharp within reach. Only the long dark hallway . . . and Death riding the air at the other end.

"You would challenge me?" Lothos hissed.

Pike charged Lothos from behind. Andy tried to stop him, but it was too late.

Lothos slammed Pike back against the wall without even looking at him. His vampire eyes were blazing, and they were still locked on Buffy.

"I'll rip the flesh from your stinking bones!" Lothos swore. "All of you!"

He looked back at the frightened students who cowered there in the gym, and his voice rose furiously.

"I am immortal! I am invincible!"

"I am so sure," Buffy said.

Lothos roared. Savagely he charged Buffy, his feet hardly skimming the ground as he raced down the hall.

He was upon her in one fraction of an instant.

In one quick motion, Buffy spun, landed on her feet, and thrust her palm out toward his chest. Lothos stopped cold.

The silence was endless and terrifying.

Buffy looked directly into his eyes, into the raw, mangled madness of his face.

Lothos seemed strangely frozen, his eyes wide and shocked, as he stared down at himself.

Sticking out of the middle of his chest was a small eraser attached to the end of a number-two pencil.

Unsteadily he took a step back, gazing at Buffy. On his charred features, the semblance of an expression settled deep into his oozing flesh.

It looked almost like respect.

Buffy stared back at him calmly. Her look was unfathomable.

Lothos blinked several times.

And then he smiled, graciously.

"Merrick was right. You are . . . a resource-ful woman."

Heavily he fell back, propped up against a row of lockers. Leaning on the row across from him, Buffy, too, slid down onto the floor. For a long moment, the two of them sat there together. Then Lothos looked down at his chest once more, and again his eyes lifted to Buffy.

"It doesn't . . . hurt . . . as much as I had imagined."

His eyes closed. . . .

As Lothos took his final breath, centuries of life coursed through him and shuddered slowly to an end.

Pike lay on the floor at the other end of the hall. Silently he watched Buffy.

Buffy didn't look back at him.

She simply sat there, staring into space.

37

In the bright light of morning, the gym lay in shambles. Police cars clustered thick in the parking lot, and medical teams tirelessly tended the wounded. For the reporters, it was a field day. For the seniors of Hemery High, it was a special memory that no one cared much to remember.

Like most morbid topics, the story—or at least the media's version of it—was fascinating for a while.

"The death toll now reaches twelve and a half in the tragedy of Hemery High School. It was at the senior dance five days ago that the school was beset by a roving gang of crack-

179

crazed gunmen. Survivors say some two hundred of the ruffians laid the school gym under a kind of siege, claiming several lives in the process. Said one administrator, 'Things here will never be the same.'"

But they were.

Within days, students walked the same hallways, holding their books the same way, talking about the same old things.

In the classrooms, they passed notes, yawned, and fell asleep.

In the mall, they window-shopped, sucked on Slurpies, laughed with their friends, and dreamed of summer vacation.

Kimberly dived gracefully into the cool, blue water of the swimming pool, coming up again on the other side. She climbed out and joined Jeffrey, Jennifer, and two new friends as they lay sunning in her backyard. They had all bought new swimsuits for the occasion, and their noses were all painted with fluorescent zinc.

"She was even crazier after that," Jennifer was saying as Kimberly walked up. "I mean it, you wouldn't even have recognized her."

"Buffy?" Kimberly guessed.

As Jennifer nodded, Kimberly wrinkled her nose in distaste.

"She didn't even hardly talk to anyone in school," Jennifer went on. "Didn't even show up for graduation. The worst is, her parents—this is true—her parents were gonna send her to the Bahamas for graduation, and she refused. True story."

"She said she didn't want to go." Kimberly looked thoroughly disgusted. "It is to vomit."

From one of the chairs a boy looked up, interested in spite of the girls' attitudes.

"Well, where is she now?" he asked.

38

In the deep quiet of evening, shadows oozed slowly along the ground. As the distant hills began to fade beyond a veil of twilight, a low wind crept suddenly through the trees, stirring their branches with a restless sigh.

Buffy led the way confidently up a long, stone drive. She was wearing a skirt, with an old sports jacket and sneakers. She glanced back at Pike, adjusting the baseball cap that sat backward on her head, and then she shifted her knapsack from one hand to the other.

"I didn't say it was a bad idea," Pike insisted, catching up to her. "I just said the timing was off. We could maybe wait till later."

"Don't be such a fraidy-cat," Buffy said.

"Who's afraid? Besides me, I mean."

"We've come all this way. We just have to check it out. I got a hunch."

"You're the boss, Boss. I just thought maybe we should wait."

Buffy stopped at the large, elaborately carved door. She gazed at it for a moment, then turned to Pike.

"Trust me."

She lifted the doorknocker, a huge iron monstrosity gripped in a gargoyle's mouth. As she pounded it against the heavy wood of the door, the sound echoed hollowly, back and back through old, forgotten chambers.

Pike and Buffy lifted their heads, gazing up at the castle that towered above them.

They saw its ancient stone walls rising out of the craggy hill, its lonely battlements and turrets hiding secrets, the last, fading glimpse of its terrifying silhouette etched sharply against the oncoming darkness.

And as the two of them stood there, side by side, night fell at last, drenching them both in the sallow light of the rising moon.

About the Author

Richie Tankersley Cusick loves vampires. She reads books and watches movies about them and she is convinced they really exist. Richie enjoys writing when it is rainy and gloomy outside, and likes to have a spooky soundtrack playing in the background. She writes at a desk which originally belonged to a funeral director in the 1800s and which she believes is haunted. Halloween is one of her favorite holidays. She and her husband decorate the entire house, which includes having a body laid out in state in the parlor, lifesize models of Frankenstein's monster, the figure of Death to keep watch, and a scary costume for Hannah, their dog. A neighbor recently told them that a previous owner of the house was feared by all of the neighborhood kids and no one would go to the house on Halloween.

Richie is the author of *Vampire, Fatal Secrets,* and *The Mall* (coming in mid-September 1992). She and her husband, Rick, live outside Kansas City, where she is currently at work on her next novel.